Pleasure Extraordinaire

Pleasure Extraordinaire

2

LIV BENNETT

I'm pursued by two brothers. Two beautiful, powerful men with dreadful secrets and gloomy pasts.

One sets me free, the other tries to trap me. One is the light in the darkness; the other is the darkness itself. Yet they have one common wish in their hearts. Seeing Michael destroyed.

But, I might be the one getting burned in the end.

The Awakening

Taylor, Adam, and I climb into the stretch limousine Michael sent for us for the engagement party he's organizing for Chloe and her boyfriend. Even though I now own a new metallic-white Audi Q5 that drives like a dream, I prefer not to be behind the wheel tonight because I'm a nervous wreck about the upcoming hours.

I slide beside Edric while Taylor and Adam get the seats across us. Edric offers his hand to

Taylor while his eyes are plastered on Adam. "Wow, you both are a delight to look at. I'm sure you'll make some absolutely gorgeous babies."

I jerk my head toward Taylor to see if Edric's words hurt her. They'd hurt me if I'd gone through what she did, but she smiles almost shyly and looks up at Adam. I have to roll my eyes and focus my attention on somewhere else, because the two seem to be getting into some kind of hypnosis session with their lovey-dovey stare, and I'd rather not be exposed to it.

Edric nudges my elbow, leaning to my ear, but his voice is loud when he says, "Why the hell haven't you told me about the existence of such a sexy guy in your family? Does he have a single brother or a cousin who looks like him?"

Right! How could I forget Adam is a magnet for any woman and apparently gay guys too? Before I can tell Edric to shut up and mind his own business, I hear Adam laughing.

"I have four crazy sisters whom I'd readily exchange for a brother or two. But I've got none. No cousins either."

"Shoot." Edric waves his hand toward him, his cheeks flushing, making him look absolutely adorable.

"Do you know anything about Chloe's soon-to-be fiancé?" I ask in an attempt to change the topic.

"Of course, I do. It's not just my job. His name is all over the Internet. His father, Clark Berenson, used to own the Berensons Country Club Taylor and Adam are now converting into a residential area under Michael's contract. They were never on good terms before the sale and it got even worse afterwards. You have no idea how furious Michael was when he found out Chloe was dating his enemy's son."

"Oh. But that's water under the bridge now, right? Otherwise Michael wouldn't want to host the engagement party at his house," I point out. Taylor is intently listening to our conversation, and I have an idea why. She once told me she was concerned about Chloe's unusual friendliness toward Adam, but the news about her engagement plans must have taken that worry out of Taylor's heart.

"If there's one thing you should learn about powerful men—" Edric says, pulling me out of my thoughts. "—it is that they don't forget or let go of things as easily as an ordinary person would do.

He's still not given up on the hope of Chloe breaking up with Dylan."

I shift in my seat, trying to find a comfortable position in the red, satin dress I'm wearing, hoping it won't tear apart with my moves. It cost five thousand dollars; it should survive at least today for the amount paid for it. "If you ask me, he's right to hope so. I wouldn't trust my daughter to my competition's son, either."

"I'm glad you're on the same side with Michael on this matter. That's the right attitude to have as his girlfriend." Edric laughs, elbowing me.

I blink several times, uncomfortable by the title Edric labeled my relationship with Michael and work hard to cover up my uneasiness. To my rescue, the car pulls up and the doors open on both sides.

I look out of the door to study the immense mansion ahead of me. I've never been to Michael's house. Hell, I've never seen even a picture of it. It's so intimidatingly large, I'm sure running around the entire building would count as a marathon. As soon as I get out, Edric whispers in my ear, "Lindsay, can I have a word with you about the new project?"

I glance at him, frowning, then at Taylor and Adam. "You guys go ahead. I'll see you in a minute."

After Taylor and Adam disappear behind the majestic French doors of the house, Edric grabs me gently by the elbow and guides me to a corner, where we can be alone without people bustling around us.

"What's the problem" I ask, suspicious about his need to be discreet about our conversation. Is it about Michael or the contract?

"I received your bill from Pleasure Extraordinaire earlier today."

I cringe at having to talk about my sexual life with a colleague I barely know. "Was it very expensive?"

"Doesn't matter. It's pennies for Michael, but hey, two escorts in one afternoon? You know how to use Michael's money on good deeds, or should I say dudes?" He winks with a naughty smile flashing across his lips.

Two escorts? "There must be a mistake. I was with one only." I immediately remember that horrible day, where Zane came close to death for licking coconut oil off of me, then paid me a surprise visit to deliver his incomplete service. As much as I enjoyed our sex to the point that I flew to the moon and back with the orgasm shooting in me, I felt disgusted for allowing Michael's son to use me that way. Where did my work ethic go?

A blue sports car pulls up, and Zane gets out of it with elegance only he can have, wearing an expensive black tux. He looks around with confidence bursting out of his entire demeanor, as if he's the only person to be paid attention to in the entire town. He wouldn't be completely wrong about it. His beauty and the pure carnality pouring out of every inch of his body is making my sex pulse as the memories of him taking me mercilessly fill my mind.

Gaping at him, with my mouth popped open no less, I begin doubting myself at the correctness of my memory of that day. Why would a man with his exquisiteness and power want to be my escort for an afternoon? The answer to that isn't difficult actually, considering my fake relationship with his father. He just wanted to taste the forbidden fruit. That can be the only reason for his desire for me. And now that he got what he wanted, he won't waste a second glance at me.

Edric disrupts my thoughts by lifting his

hand right up to my face, waving it to pull me back from the dirty images of that afternoon at my home that were floating in my mind. "Hey, I get it. They were simply too good to choose just one, so you went with both. I'd do the same if I was you, but unfortunately they don't serve gays. At least not yet."

I can barely listen to Edric while I watch Zane opening the door of the passenger side of his car. A beautiful woman, most likely a fashion model with her long legs and size-zero body, holds out her hand for Zane to grab and help her out. I struggle to keep the disappointment that freezes my heart on the spot, when I see the girl sliding her slim arms around Zane's waist while he kisses her lips with the intimacy of a long-time lover.

"Seriously," I mutter. "I was only with one escort." I tear my eyes away from the painful sight of Zane sharing a deep kiss with that woman and focus myself on my conversation with Edric so I can keep my sanity.

Mr. Ice charged me for two men. Yes, that information should be powerful enough to divert my attention. I should feel angry, and yes, I am indeed. That son of a bitch. Then it occurs to me. He must have charged for the blow job I gave to him. My gesture was mostly for his pleasure, to help him get his release. But no, he has to get paid for being blown off. It's working. My heart is back to pumping fast with anger at Mr. Ice. "How much was it in total?"

I hardly notice Zane and his date strolling through the front doors. As much as I'm angry with Mr. Ice, a part of me feels glad at his fraud for keeping my mind off Zane.

"Not much. Thirty-three hundred. Like I said, it's nothing for Michael. Don't you worry your beautiful head about those insignificant details."

"That much money?" I could have hired JJ for that amount if I knew I'd get half the service I was supposed to get with two men. The longer I think about Mr. Ice's rudeness, the more rage fills me up. He's a liar and opportunist to twist the bill of a client this way. Just because Michael happens to have a lot of money doesn't give anyone right to exploit him.

I hear Michael calling for me and I turn to see him getting out of a limo parked behind Zane's car.

"I'll see you later," I tell to Edric and head toward Michael, nearly running, because seeing

Michael's sunshine face is a pull to my usually depressed, disappointed, and angry self. "Hey, Michael. So nice to see you."

He spreads his arms open and wraps them around me when I'm in front of him. "Had I known I'd be welcomed like this, I'd drive over to your place and pick you up myself." Leaning down, he brushes my cheek with a smooth kiss for a brief second. I hear the click of a camera from a distance at the moment of his kiss, but I don't see anyone when I pull back and scan around.

"I had an urgent meeting with one of the associates," Michael adds.

"Are you seriously giving me an excuse for sending a limousine to have me picked up?"

He holds my hand, directing me back to the stairs. A couple walks past us, turning only briefly to greet Michael. I squeeze my hand around his as we stroll toward the front door that a security guard holds open for us.

We don't talk; we don't even look at each other in the elevator that takes us to the salon where the party is held. My heart shoots up as we step out of the cab and head toward the doors of the salon. If no one knew about our relationship, they'll know it now. His family, friends, employees, business partners, and the worst of all: the media. Edric mentioned to me a few days ago; they had invited reporters from Hawkins' Media to get our pictures taken to be published in magazines and on the Internet.

Just before the doorman waiting in front of the salon opens the doors for us to enter, Michael lifts my hands to his lips, with a reassuring smile on his face, and stares at my eyes pointedly. "It's all right. They're all friends, and family, and people who work for me. I'll introduce you to some of my business associates, and then we'll get our pictures taken. That'll be it."

Once the word, "Okay," escapes my mouth, Michael nods to the doorman, and he opens the door for us. I'm momentarily blinded by the flash of lights as we make our grand entrance. I'm only dating Michael. I'm not even his girlfriend, but the intense attention we get from the guests tells me just the opposite. As if the engagement party is thrown for us.

Holding tightly onto Michael's hand and breathing deeply, I take hesitant steps toward the ocean of people. Just friends, family and people who work for Michael make easily three-four-hundred people, because the majestic salon is filled up to the brim with the sheer number of guests.

If I felt nervous before entering, now I'm suffocating with fear. It's not the first time my photograph will be taken by the media, but never have I felt so exposed before so many eyes that are staring at me with curiosity, and even condemnation, as if they've seen through my little role play as Michael's date.

Whatever Edric might have claimed about my relationship with Michael to prove that this isn't a lie and that Michael and I are just dating and getting to know each other, what I'm doing here is indeed a lie. Michael might have taken me out on a date, but we both know it wasn't a real date that might have led up to romance. And worse yet, it's not even a genuine help to a friend. I'm getting paid for it.

My mouth goes dry, and I feel blood draining out of me. Working hard to breathe in and out long and evenly so I am able to walk straight, I smile at the cameras pointing at me. Not even Michael gets half the attention the media untactfully showers on me.

At one point, upon the request of one of the

reporters, Michael leaves my hand so the photographers take more of my pictures, like they haven't already had enough to fill up the memory cards of their cameras.

My eyes look for Taylor in the crowd so I can feel a bit of familiarity in this eccentric situation, and when I spot her, she grins at me with warmth and joy. Is she enjoying the party? Sure, she'll have a chance to get to know people who hold the ties to the State's economy and maybe spread the name of her construction company. At least, my little deceit might help her get more clients. Feeling a little calmer and more in control of my body, I direct my gaze at the cameras and flash a broad smile, one of which I've practiced a lot around the time my name became famous as Iron Slap.

Edric comes beside me, discreetly whispering in my ear that one of the reporters requested to have a private interview with me about my relationship with Michael. I try my best not to look at him in horror as I relay him my acceptance.

After the long, sweat-inducing photo session is over, Edric guides me to a relatively secluded corner, only occupied with two men, whom I assume are responsible for security. As soon as I'm introduced to the reporter, a middle-aged, brunette lady, Edric leaves us alone.

I sit cautiously on the chair opposite the reporter and cross my legs, settling my hands in loose fists on my lap. She bombards me with questions which I can answer easily and with full honesty, like what my first reaction was when I met Michael, whether it was attraction at first sight, whether I thought of making a move during the period where I didn't hear anything from Michael after our first meeting.

Despite my initial horror, I find myself explaining more than her questions are aimed at, going into detail about my fascination with Michael's looks, gentleness, care, and diligence when it comes to his work. All in all, nothing comes out of my mouth is smeared with lies, and I have a nagging suspicion that Michael went through her questions before allowing her to do the interview.

Michael shows up the second the reporter ends the interview and asks her to send the article to him prior to publishing it. When she's gone, Michael holds out his hand to help me to my feet and leaves a quick kiss on my cheek. That's the second kiss in half an hour. Should I be worried about his unusual kiss attack? I don't mutter that thought.

"Thanks for the interview. I haven't felt this flattered in years," he says, smiling.

"Have you been listening?" I feel my cheeks turn hot at his playful smile.

He nods, broadening his smile.

"You should know, everything I said is my true feelings about you."

"I know. I had no idea I had such an effect on women."

"Yeah, right. Like I'll believe that." I roll my eyes, slamming into him with my shoulder playfully. I'm sure Zane doesn't have a tenth of Michael's humility when it comes to his looks. Oh, Zane. Perhaps it's a good thing he's with another woman, so I can put forth a serious effort to take him out of my mind and forget about the hot and sweaty minutes we shared in my apartment.

Michael holds my hand and points with his head toward the door. "Shall we?"

With a renewed confidence, I follow suit, and this time I show up at the salon with more confidence and determination to enjoy the party. Michael guides me through the mass of people, stopping practically every second to shake hands and introduce me.

I smile and try to exchange a few words of greetings with the guests, but after half an hour of repeating the same thing, my facial muscles begin to hurt for having been pulled up for so long, and my stomach growls with hunger. I'm glad for the live music and the noise of people chatting around me for covering up the embarrassing proof of my hunger.

To keep myself from dying of complete boredom while Michael exchanges niceties with the guests, I dedicate myself to analyzing the dresses the ladies chose to wear for this luscious party. After red, the colors of gold and silver seem to be in trend and also the shorter the better for the skirts.

After an hour of shaking hands and rinse-and-repeat introductions, we finally reach our table, where Taylor and Adam are also sitting. Michael excuses himself to continue involving himself with his guests, and I plop my already tired body into the chair beside Taylor and grab a piece of the pastry to calm my raging stomach.

"This party is unreal," Taylor whispers to my ear. "How are you doing?"

"All right, I guess. Have you met anyone interesting?"

"Yeah. Dylan Berenson's parents."

"Did you find out why they sold the Country Club? I thought golf is a permanent money-making machine, since wealthy men love hanging out with their wealthy fellows."

Taylor shrugs. "Don't ask me." Then she turns to Adam, who is busying himself with his phone. "Have you heard anything about why the Berensons sold the Country Club?"

Adam just shrugs, keeping his eyes locked on his phone. "I'm not sure, but according to the rumors, some drug lords used it as their location to make deals. Once the police found it out, they canceled the liquor license of the club. That was the beginning of the end, I guess."

What a way to end a successful business? Even one of the safest businesses can flip unexpectedly. Which makes me feel grateful for having decided to accept Michael's offer in exchange for money. Just like I lost my job without actually being at fault after suing the supervisor who tried to harass me sexually, Clark Berenson lost his business because of other people's misconduct.

"What are you looking at?" I hear Taylor asking Adam, but my mind is busy with feeling compassion for the Berenson family and contemplating people who ruin others' livelihood.

Through the line of people, I glance at Chloe and her fiancé Dylan. Both being gorgeous and glamorous, they make an eye-catching couple. Yet, I'm failing to see any passion or intimate glances between the two. They hold hands, yes, but nothing else in their behavior proves they're going through the first step of uniting their lives. Perhaps, they're well-versed on how to behave when surrounded by an immense number of people and cameras. If acting distant is the norm, then I should be happy about how I act with Michael, because he and I react the same way to each other as Chloe and Dylan.

I see Zane and his date approaching Chloe, and soon Chloe is flashing ear-to-ear grins to her brother. Well, that, too, I'd do exactly the same if Zane was hugging me tightly with his sturdy body as he's hugging Chloe.

Doing my best to ignore my resentful feelings toward him, I wonder where Chloe's other brother is. The only information I know about Christian

Hawkins is that he's the youngest among the three and also the most private. That's why I never got to see any pictures of him from any mainstream media. That and the lack of interest from my side to waste useful time on nonsense gossip about celebrities.

But now, sitting here, wondering who among the hundreds of people is the youngest Hawkins, I feel dumb for not going through at a few magazines to know how he looks.

The music band stops playing, and I hear Michael's soothing voice over the microphone. "Ladies and gentlemen." He pauses, perhaps waiting for the guests to turn their attention to him. "I can't thank you enough for being with me during one of the worst days of my life." A roar of laughter takes over the salon at Michael's sarcasm. "Aside from sickness or death in the family, I think giving his daughter away is the hardest thing a father can face.

Enjoying Michael's light and warm confessions, I turn to Taylor and Adam and see their faces long with dolefulness. Of course, as parents of a deceased daughter they'll not enjoy Michael's jokes. I reach up and cover Taylor's hand on the table, wishing they'll have another child much sooner rather than later.

"If it wasn't for the man Chloe chose to marry, I'd have to speak to the Governor to push up the legal age to marry to fifty-five." Michael holds up his hand toward Chloe in the middle of the salon, and she walks through the crowd toward the stage, with her boyfriend behind her.

Once the young couple is on the stage, taking their places on each side of Michael, people begin clasping hands. Michael raves about his soon-to-be son-in-law's success in business for minutes to come, and I can't help but feel my attention being drawn to somewhere else. To Michael's biological son, Zane. His girlfriend is nowhere to be seen—I wish she'd vanish altogether, but I shouldn't be harsh to someone for falling for the Adonis in flesh and blood.

Much to my bad luck, Zane reciprocates my stare, cocking his head to the side while the corner of his eyes crinkles with a daring smile. I drop my gaze to the table before me, wishing he hadn't noticed my blatant ogling, and when I look back up, I see him strolling toward me, ignoring the people around.

Shit. If he mentions anything about Saturday afternoon, Taylor will get a whiff and then start asking question. That'll be the end of everything related to my silence about the contract. No, no, I tell myself. He won't speak anything about that embarrassing encounter.

"Adam, Taylor." Zane nods and shake their hands, as the gentleman as he can be, and then settles in the chair next to me.

Everything else, the guests, Michael's talk, Taylor on my other side, lose their significance in a matter of seconds as I feel Zane's arm brushing mine for a brief second. I hold my breath and concentrate on the napkin in my hands in an effort to stifle the shivering the close distance between us is giving me. It's an impossible task, though, because the memories of him wrapping his hands around my body, flipping me over, and bending me down on the arm of the couch flood my mind, and my sex pulses with the need to be stretched by his manhood again.

Pulling the chair closer to mine, Zane leans in and whispers in my ear, "Bla, bla, bla."

As if I wasn't already aroused, his lips brush my skin and the hair on my nape jumps up at the touch of his lips and the seductiveness of his deep voice. I gasp, unable to do anything else, wishing his girlfriend would come and save me from him, or I'm sure Taylor or another guest will see his effect on me. Worse, he'll realize I turn into a puddle of goo at his mere presence.

"What?" I ask, tilting my head slightly toward him, willing my sex to stop interfering with my brain.

"My father, the actor."

I shake my head to convey to him my confusion, glancing up at his eyes briefly. Without my control, my tongue brushes my lips to moisten them, and I notice Zane's face lightening up with a seductive smile.

"Why do you say that?" I mumble each word with difficulty like a drunken person would speak.

"His publicist jotted down his speech for him."

I turn my attention back to Michael, who's still on the stage in front of the microphone while embracing Chloe and Dylan under each arm. "That's not true."

"Being a father to a daughter is something unique, something extraordinary," Michael says. "I don't mean any disrespect to my sons. I wouldn't change them for the world, but when I held Chloe in my arms the first time on the day of her birth, she stared at me intently, as if she knew who I was. My heart changed permanently as I realize who she was. The real owner of my heart. Her birth gave me reason to be the best person and father I can be, make the world a better place for her, and make her proud of me."

Zane smirks. His face looks amused and pained at the same time. "Lies, all lies. He was on a business trip the day Chloe was born. The first time he saw her was when she was already five months old. Not just that, during her first year, he visited her only three times, and maybe half an hour at each visit. He didn't care about us in the least when we were kids. He doesn't care about us now, either."

I'm having difficulty picturing Michael as a heartless father. He's sweet and thoughtful to say the least. "How can you say that about your father?"

"Because, I know him. He's not the person you think he is. He's mastered his role as a caring gentleman after years of practicing. Don't fall for his games. Nobody with a loving heart and good intentions can even dream about the power and money he owns. These're all his games, and we're all his puppets. Chloe, you, me. Even the governor can't pass laws if my father is against them, because he's threatened to close down his business in California and move to another state, leaving thousands of people unemployed."

I analyze Zane's cold expression and his intent eyes for a clue to his lie, or at least a motivation behind his smear campaign. "If he's such a bad person as you make him out to be, then why are you working for him? Why don't you run from him as far away as you can?"

"As if it's slightly possible. He won't let me be free. I'm the equivalent of a slave to him. When I finished college and told him I wanted to found my own company, do my own business, he told me he'd use everything in his power for me to fail and end up on the streets if I don't follow his steps and do as he orders. You might be under contract with him for a year; I'm signed up for a lifetime."

"I'd like to form my own opinion about people," I finally say, hoping this weird conversation will end. Now I really want his girlfriend to come and rescue me from him.

He arches an eyebrow, sizing me up and down with a critical expression playing in his eyes and nods. "Sure, but be very careful. Make sure to not do anything beyond what's written on your contract, because once he sees you cave in to one thing, he won't stop demanding more."

What is he talking about now? What can Michael demand from me beyond the contract? It's not like he'll serve me to his business partners for their sexual pleasures. He might have lots of money, but not that kind of power to break the laws at his will. "I'll keep that in mind," I snap and turn ahead to continue watching Michael.

He's talking about a humorous memory of him together with Chloe when she was six, and both Chloe and Dylan are laughing at his words. That memory can't be a lie. Chloe's laughter can't be fake. Or? I thought I was good at catching when a person lies, but I might have to reconsider my ability.

Edric appears and bows down between me and Zane to whisper something into his ear. I can make out only the: "You're expected on the stage," part and look up at Zane as he stands, pushing his chair back.

He reaches for my shoulder and not so gently squeezes it before saying, "work is waiting," to my ear. I watch him idly as he slowly walks away and makes it to the stage, next to his father, his sister, his soon-to-be in-law and ... Mr. Icc.

Wait! What's Mr. Ice doing on the stage?

He doesn't have any place there with Michael's family unless he's a bodyguard or some sort of personnel responsible for the stage equipment. Which I highly doubt, considering the millions he must be making with his brothel business.

"Taylor, do you know the blond guy next to Michael?" I ask.

"Don't you know? That's Chris Hawkins. Michael's youngest child," Taylor informs, and I barely tear my eyes from Mr. Ice to face Taylor.

"Are we talking about the same guy? I thought his name was Ace Preston."

"Oh, yeah. Ace is his middle name. Preston is his deceased mother's maiden name. According to the rumors, Michael disowned him when he turned eighteen. That's why Chris changed his name to Preston. But according to the other rumors, Michael is a gay, but that can't be true since you're dating him. I think Ace uses his mother's last name to honor her."

"Seriously?" My head swivels back and forth between Taylor and the stage, but I can't find it in me to look up at Ace and Zane, the two brothers whose penises I got too intimate with. Nothing can take away the feeling of dirtiness taking me over right now, for sleeping with two men who came out of the same womb. It's wrong on so many levels, I can't even wrap my head around how I couldn't see it.

Watching them on the stage while they're patting each other's shoulders, laughing together, and exchanging words of brotherly love in front of hundreds of people makes my stomach revolt with disgust for letting them play with me like a fool. What kind of sick game have they pulled me into?

Especially Ace.

He knew his brother was the escort I'd spend my Saturday afternoon with, yet still, he didn't refrain from massaging and fingering my privates. Now I'm sure it was all Ace's idea to use coconut oil on me. As Zane's brother, he must have known about his allergies and still smeared it all over my vagina. Deliberately lying to me about the oil being Zane's choice.

I have no idea why he'd do such a horrible thing to his own brother. For all I know, they're a bunch of spoiled brats, getting a kick out of dirty tricks, the more dangerous the better.

Ace nearly came to killing his brother, yet now he looks at him with love and respect, as if Zane is his best friend, his idol, his everything. The same goes for Zane and every other member of the family. Zane was right. They're brilliant actors, the kind you can only see among Oscar award winners.

I feel my stomach rolling over with disgust. Perhaps lying is a common practice, even expected in this world of money and power. Phony bodies can host phony souls only. No one would want to see a family fighting with each other. Even if it's just pretending, a happy-looking group of people must be what's required among these people. Perhaps that's the only thing they're capable of perceiving. Hatred is ugly, especially against a family member, and god forbid if the precious eyes of these wealthy and powerful mass get exposed to the ugliness of the world.

What am I doing here? I have no place among them, yet, as if being part of their wicked show isn't enough, I'm pulling Taylor with me into their repulsive lives.

I want to jump up from my chair and run as fast as I can, but I shift and straighten my dress slowly, before getting on my feet.

"Where are you going?" Taylor asks, eyeing

me curiously.

"I don't feel good," which is true. "I think I'll go home."

"What do you have?" She stands with me.

"I don't know. My stomach feels weird."

"Oh, okay. I'll go with you."

I don't decline her offer, because the faster she's out of here with me, the less she'll be exposed to the poisonous air these children of evil breathe out. Adam joins us too, and we pass among tables under the curious eyes of the guests and head to the door.

Before we can reach the door, though, Edric shows up, grabbing my elbow. "Hey, girl. Where are you going?" he asks with a hint of worry in his voice.

"Home. I'm not feeling good."

"What is it? If it's headache or stomachache, I have boxes of painkillers in the car."

I sigh, trying to think of a credible yet honest way to convince Edric that I won't be able to stay for the rest of the party, but such a way is impossible to find unless I tell him the truth. "I'll be right back," I say to Taylor and Adam and walk to an isolated corner with Edric.

Edric glances around, his eyebrows pulled together, and then turns to me. "You're making me worried. Is it Zane? I saw you two chatting. What'd he say?"

"What didn't he say?" I face him with frustration, biting my lower lip with anger.

"Will you finally tell me what's going on?"

"Lots of things, but it all boils down to what a liar Michael is, that he's just a show, doesn't actually care about Chloe or his other kids."

Edric's expression softens visibly as he glances at me. "You should take Zane's words about his father with grain of salt, because he's mad at him for not retiring this year and leaving the control of all his companies to Zane as he'd promised. Michael might be a workaholic, but he loves his children just like any other father and would do anything to protect them and give them the lives that only a few can afford. He came from poverty. Because of that, I guess, he fears he or his family will go back to those difficult days in his past. He sleeps only four hours daily. The rest of the time is dedicated to work so his family is well off. I've worked for Michael for fifteen years, and if

I'd come across any misbehavior or unethical conduct from his side, I'd resign without blinking an eye. He's just a driven man with fantastic instincts about money and investment. Nothing else."

"I don't know." I shrug my irritation away. "You might be right. I haven't observed anything unusual or malicious from Michael. He has been nothing but sweet and supportive since the day I met him."

On the other hand, Zane took advantage of me sexually the minute he figured out I was a client at Pleasure Extraordinaire. He's the real poison here, not Michael. And if it's true that he was planning to take over Michael's companies, he must be mightily pissed off for having to wait longer to hold the reins of one of the most profitable enterprises of the nation. I shouldn't let people get into me so easily, especially people with ulterior motives, like Zane. I'll be better off keeping my contact with him and his brother to a bare minimum if I want to stay sane.

"Exactly. Michael is an old soul," Edric continues. "He has seen the world at its worst. However, Zane grew up having everything he could think of and not having to worry about a damn thing in his life. He can be very manipulative when he doesn't get what he wants. Just be very careful around him, don't let him fill your mind with lies, and you'll be fine."

"Thanks, Edric. I was feeling really down. I guess I'll have to improve my people skills to weed out liars."

"It's not an easy task, but you'll get there eventually."

Even though talking with Edric calms my agitated nerves, I still don't want to stay at the party for the rest of the evening. But I guess, in the eyes of other guests, if I disappear before the party officially starts, that won't look good for me as Michael's date, and I did promise him I'll be his date for tonight.

When I try and explain to Taylor that I changed my mind about leaving, she looks up at Adam, and just like that, they walk back to our table with me. It feels good to have people who won't complain about my ups and downs.

A few minutes after we settle back into our chairs, the servers begin bustling around to serve our plates and drinks. The sight of the exquisite food makes me feel glad to have changed my mind about staying.

Michael remains at the table with his children and Dylan's parents, while an elderly couple accompanies us at our table. I nearly come to crying when I see Taylor's face beam with hope as the lady with bright white hair talks about her fair share of miscarriages before bringing five healthy kids into the world.

After the dessert, Michael spends a few minutes at our table, discussing some work-related things about the construction project with Taylor and Adam, proving Edric correct about his workaholic attitude for talking about work during a party dedicated to his daughter. Then he takes me for a couple of rounds of dancing.

I let myself relax in his arms as we swirl on the dance floor, marveling at his energy and enthusiasm. I wonder about his lover, whether he's here among the guests, perhaps eyeing us with jealousy and resentment for not being able to dance with the man he loves and instead watching him in the arms of another person. Despite my curiosity, I don't ask Michael about his lover, not wanting to deepen his wounds. It's his night as a father; he should enjoy it to the full and not be reminded of what he's missing in his life.

I catch both Zane and Ace glaring at us more than a couple of times, but ignore their glowers. They're nothing but two lost souls, taking extra pleasure from using people for their satisfaction without caring about if they hurt them in the process or not.

I figure the best way to take revenge on egotistical brats is to behave as if they don't exist and that their presence is no more significant than that of nonliving things. So, I just do exactly that. Whenever my eyes get caught with Zane's, I laugh loudly at something Michael says and turn my gaze back to Michael, brushing off my thrumming heartbeats. If I accidentally encounter Ace's death glint on me, I make it my purpose to not spend more than a few seconds before I land my eyes on something more interesting, say the empty glasses on a table or even the creamy texture of the walls, making sure to not display any emotion on my face.

Yet, my ploy seems to have its limits, because when Ace comes forth and requests the next dance from Michael—and Michael happily complies—I can't keep my regard emotionless and distant. Not when he's so close and exhaling his hot breath on my face. Not when he's holding my hand so tightly as if promising me he'll never let me go. Not when the grip of his fingers on my hip sends jolts of electricity all over my body.

Ahh, fuck the Hawkins brothers. I was more satisfied with my life before them, without having any man in my life, than now with two men attempting to get me on all fours at the first opportunity.

"Have you sworn off talking to me?" Ace asks after a long minute of silence.

"I usually keep my interaction with liars to the bare minimum," I retort, scowling to channel my loathing to him, and it seems it's working because his usually blank face is beaming with a hint of uneasiness. Good.

"I didn't lie to you."

I roll my eyes in effect, dropping my gaze to his chest to keep my boiling anger in control, for if I continue looking at his hypocritical face, I might just throw up.

"I deserve some benefit of doubt," he claims.

"Not when someone came close to getting hurt because of you."

"What can I do to make you believe that it

wasn't my idea to apply coconut on you, and I just did what was requested?"

I shake my head and shrug my shoulders. "It's a hopeless case for you because there's nothing you can do to make me believe you unless you prove it. If you can't, I suggest you not tire yourself with empty words."

"Look at me. Look at my eyes." He pulls his hand that's holding my hip and reaches for my chin to lift my gaze up at his face. "It's not the first time Zane had a client over at PE. In fact, he's been working as an external contractor for longer than three months, and I've done nothing to sabotage his work or his health. I'd never do anything dangerous to my employees, not even if he's the brother I have and hate." His eyebrows rise and his eyes grow with sadness, or something that resembles it, and I wish my instincts are correct and he's being honest with me. But how can I trust my hunch about him or his family anymore, now that I know they're better than professional actors when it comes to deceiving others?

He keeps his fingers under my chin and slowly runs his thumb right below my lower lip, meanwhile casting his beautiful, blue eyes into the abyss of my soul. "I didn't do it. I had no reason to.

Well, I won't deny the fact that I felt jealous of him for securing a rendezvous with you, but I'd never put his life in danger for anything. If I felt it'd be wrong for him to be with you, I'd simply cancel his request, and that'd be the end of the arrangement."

He was feeling jealous of Zane? That's news to me. I reach for his hand holding my chin to stop him from causing goose bumps on my skin. Taking advantage of the situation, he laces his fingers through mine and rests my hand on his chest for a brief moment before placing it back on his shoulder.

"I want to believe you," I confess. "I really do, but then if you didn't type the coconut thing on the database, who did? Zane? It doesn't make any sense."

"I hired someone to look into it and to see if it was someone among my employees. No one knew about Zane's allergy to coconut because he hadn't mentioned anything about it on his profile. Even I had no idea he had such a rare allergy, as ridiculous as it may sound. So, this leaves only Zane or an outsider as the suspect. You're right on one point, though. Zane trying to kill himself doesn't make sense."

"I don't know." I actually do, and I think I believe him. Accepting his argument is easier on my heart, I admit.

"Zane hasn't sued me for the trouble, which he had every right to do, but you're the one challenging me. What is it with you?"

"I hate liars. I don't lie myself, and I expect the same courtesy from others, and when I don't receive the same treatment, I get upset. And... and let's not forget the fact that you took advantage of me."

"I guess an apology is due for what I did to you but, to my defense, either I'd do that or I'd sign up as an escort, something I've never done before, to deal with my desire for you." His gaze changes from apologetic to scorching in a matter of seconds, and I find all my guards against him are being disarmed one by one with the temping words his eyes are conveying, without him having to open his mouth.

He digs his fingers on my hips as if to remind me where they were on Saturday afternoon. Deep inside me, thrusting and stroking. Just where I want them to be now.

Panther - ACE

Lindsay isn't a beauty in the classical sense. She's short; her body isn't slim or athletic. Her lips are disproportional; the upper one is thicker than the lower one. And, the worst of it all, she's a natural frowner. Her eyebrows are knitted closely in their natural manner, making her look upset most of the time, even though she may not be so in reality.

My first reaction to her before we exchanged words was fear. She looks like she can finish you with just one move. And, the fact that she actually killed someone with no less than a slap is simply frightening.

I saw the video of how she killed that woman. It wasn't your usual slap that makes noise and maybe hurts a little but leaves no residual effect. Lindsay's slap shoved Macey Williams from one side to the other of a five-hundred-square-foot room. If the hook hadn't been there, the severe way she crashed into the wall due to the impact of the slap would have caused her to have some serious brain damage.

That's why, whoever came up with Iron Slap as an alias for her is genius for rightly terming what Lindsay is. She's iron through and through, hard to break, even harder to defeat. Like someone you can trust during hardships and obstacles. You can be sure she'll try her darndest to protect you and stand by you without thinking for a second to analyze the downsides.

Funny, how her personality occupies my mind more than the feel of her moist vagina around my finger, or her ferocious tongue rubbing my skin. Don't get me wrong, I think about those, too. More often than I should. The way she appears so virginal in her normal state, as if she hasn't heard of the word sex in her life, then with a simple touch transforms into a wild panther, vicious and ready to take whatever she wants.

Damn me if watching her get off after I rubbed her with coconut oil, then having her attack my cock weren't the sexiest moments of my life. Even days after the event, all I can think about when I remember her lips is how they rounded my cock and sucked me ruthlessly. That's saying a lot for a man like me who has seen literally everything related to sex.

I can easily picture a life where she's using me ruthlessly for her sexual pleasure every day for the rest of my life and that, in itself, is frightening, because no woman before has aroused that feeling in me.

She's frowning again, her eyebrows two thin flat lines above her fearless eyes. A shiver crosses my torso when those eyes land on me, as if evaluating me for my strength, teasing me for my weaknesses.

I swallow and mirror her face so she can't see through the wall I build around my fragile core, one that has been shattered one too many times over the years. I don't hear the music anymore; my ears have turned deaf to anything except for her voice and her irregular breathing.

"Why did you charge me for two escorts? You had no reason to." Her voice is commanding, just like her entire demeanor. She can rule an army, and no soldier will have the balls to disobey her commands.

"I didn't want you to violate the contract you signed with Michael. What happened between us without me billing you for an extra escort would automatically qualify as a breach of contract, even if it had stayed as a secret between you and me. The last thing I want is for you to have problems due to the pleasure you receive at PE." I make sure to stress pleasure, because I love catching her by surprise, giving her no chance to restrain her emotions from flooding her face and her expression revealing all the passion and desire that must be erupting inside her. That's exactly what is happening right now. Her cheeks are glowing with a kissable touch of pink, reminding me of the moments I had her exposed. I dare smile.

The panther has awakened. Again.

My cock stirs beneath my pants. My heart throbs frantically as I remember her lips taut around my shaft, her tongue mercilessly licking my desires awake. She avenged me for the two minimal minutes I got to enjoy her pussy by playing with me as if I was a teenage virgin, trying to control my cum, ridiculing my masculinity with fingering me in my asshole. I fear if I dare cross the line again, her next sanction won't be so mild.

She shakes her head. Despite the clear blushing of her face, she won't give up, and I'm not surprised in the least. "Still, it doesn't justify the amount you charged. That much money for pleasure that you received?"

I'd have given her the full satisfaction if she hadn't yanked my hand away right before she could come. Despite that, I can't complain for the view of her fucking herself with her fingers and breaking apart uncontrollably, as if it was her first orgasm ever. That sight of her will very likely never abandon my thoughts till it's replaced by a more stunning scene. Although I highly doubt the possibility of it, Lindsay continues rendering me stunned each time I meet her and will most likely provide me with a better spectacle that'll leave me gaping and drooling. I can only hope that opportunity will present itself very soon.

I'm not a man who leaves anything to chance,

including an erotic diversion with a babe like Lindsay. "I strive for the best customer satisfaction, and I not only apologize for the inconvenience, but also would like to offer you a one-time promotion to gain back your loyalty as a customer."

Shooting me a smug look, she slides her hand ever so slowly from the top of my shoulders down to my biceps, spreading her fingers widely around my arms, as if measuring their girth. "Let's hear it."

"Have you ever had a chance to enjoy a threesome?" When her eyebrows knit further together, I add, "with two men?" I can see she's not into sharing. So panther of her.

She shakes her head. Her eyes grow large with expectation.

"Next time you pay a visit to PE, you'll receive a complimentary second escort with no additional costs. And, just to make the offer irresistible, you'll be able to choose whomever you want, including the most expensive man I employ, for free."

She blushes, raises her eyebrows, locks her eyes on mine intently, then drops them down on my chest, and I have a clue what's going through her mind.

"Yes, you may choose me as well, if you desire so," I say to answer her unvoiced question.

"Don't get your hopes high. I don't sleep with brothers," she says and releases her hands from my arms, removing her body from my hold. When I try to figure out why, I realize the band is announcing to take a break, ending the few minutes of intimacy I've enjoyed with Lindsay.

I glance down at her, not yet done with our talk. "What you had with Zane barely counts as sex. He went into a coma before he could do anything with you."

"Hasn't he told you? He came over to my apartment later that afternoon to complete his task."

That scumbag. "I wasn't informed about that."

"Well, now you know." With that, she spins around and heads toward the table where her sister sits. Zane has to ruin everything for me again. If it wasn't for him, Lindsay would choose me as the complimentary escort without a second thought. Now, however, I have to accept the defeat and let her play with whomever she wants over at PE. As much as I desire her to receive the highest of the pleasures, I have to admit, I wish it was me who could give it to her.

Keeping a straight face, I work up the courage to settle at the table beside Chloe and nod at Dylan. He seems unusually calm for a man who'll soon tie the knot. Honestly, I don't understand why he's hurrying to marry at the age of twenty four, let alone my sister. He should have waited for another ten years, at least, to make sure Chloe is the right one for him.

Actually, only a month should be enough to see she's no match for any man, thanks to Michael's ever-insistent presence in her life. If Dylan hasn't realized that during the one year they've been together, he deserves a lifelong sentence with Michael. It's not like he'll have a choice to divorce either. Whoever enters the Hawkins clan is in it for a lifetime.

Zane sends me an irritating 'I've got what you couldn't,' sneer, and I clench my fists under the table, wanting to punch that look away. How did he know Lindsay's alias? If I'd known it soon enough, I'd have tried to prevent their union. To top everything off, he had to finish it off by going to her place without prior notice. I'll have to put an end to his headstrong attitude, though I'm afraid His Majesty, Michael, will have a say on whatever I do too, and I'll wind up overlooking Zane's mistakes once again.

Zane's girlfriend's arms are around him like a snake, never leaving him for a second, but he doesn't give a damn and instead shoots rotten glances at Lindsay. He had her already; why does he bother to go after her again?

Oh, wait. I know the answer. To bother me. I have to keep my face straight not to give him further incentive to pursue Lindsay, but goddamnit if it was possible. He knows how to push my buttons and won't stop until I get into a fight with him. Which will give him the upper hand and a reason to complain to his daddy about my violence.

I signal to a server for more champagne, and she fills my glass with a hesitant move, glancing up at me with a shy smile and blushes when I thank her. Now that's a beauty with her delicate features, fit body, long legs, wavy blond hair, bright blue eyes, and perfect skin. If it was any other day, I'd led her toward the restroom and have my way with her, but today, her beauty doesn't even cause a twitch of my cock.

Despite my disinterest, I wink at her, reciprocating her gorgeous smile, knowing Zane will be observing me. As a child, he always wanted what I wanted, and as an adult he's no different. As expected, he motions with a finger toward his own glass, though it's half full, and compliments the girl's eyes.

Zane's date keeps her arms locked around his; perhaps harder this time while he's flirting with the server, as the server fills up Zane's glass, and then his date's glass with shaky hands. Before she leaves, Zane slips a business card into the pocket of her shirt over her chest and stares after her at her ass. What a jackass, but at least he's stopped eye-fucking Lindsay.

Or not?

Grabbing the hands of his date to get himself free of her hold, he stands, pushing the chair behind, and walks toward Lindsay's table.

I barely hear Chloe's words through my infuriated heartbeats. "You didn't come to Mom's anniversary," Chloe states with a worried tone in her voice.

"I went to visit her grave in the morning, but

something urgent came up in the evening. I called Michael, though. He said it was okay."

"Shhh. You're not allowed to call him by his name in public." Chloe glances around for onlookers, but no one seems to care, even Zane's date who's sitting only a foot away from us. She's too occupied with Zane's whereabouts to notice anything.

"Yes." How dare I call his Majesty by his name? In fact, I should call him my king, because that's exactly what he does; rule my life. But I shouldn't complain. Zane and Chloe have it worse than I. At least, I don't have to work for him or live in his house under his rules. As long as I keep the role of the happy son who's proud of his father on occasions like today's event, I'm off his hook. "Have you already set a wedding date?" I ask, in an attempt to distract myself from the disturbing thoughts of what Zane must be talking about with Lindsay.

"We're thinking of marrying next month in Las Vegas."

Dream on. Like Michael is ever going to allow that. Any wedding with less than a-million-dollar expenditure is a shame for him. "Have you talked to Dad about your plans?"

"No, not yet. He'll probably say no."

"Not probably, definitely is the word you're looking for."

"You're right. But it's okay. Dylan doesn't mind waiting. Do you, baby?"

Dylan, for the first time, grabs Chloe's hand and lifts it up to kiss it. "I can wait for you for an eternity."

I glance at the table where Michael is sitting with his business partners to see if he's noticed Dylan's kiss on Chloe's hand. Michael is a jealous prick, even toward his own daughter, and will easily show his real face if he sees any man showing physical affection to her. His mind has gotten more twisted over the years. I hope he'll die soon and finally leave us all alone. "Well, good luck with telling Mic—Dad, your wedding plans. Let me know if you need any help."

Chloe and Dylan stand and move to the dance floor, holding each other as if they're brother and sister, with no passion or desire readable in their behavior. They're well-versed in their behavior. Rightly so, because more than a few times Michael interfered with Chloe's classmates at college for showing interest in her.

With interference, I mean the parents' of the boys losing their jobs, houses, and money, or something just as severe.

Michael doesn't tolerate any misconduct. That's rule number one. The rule number two is he never forgives.

I turn my gaze to Zane's date and lift my glass to her, smiling to lift her spirits a bit. I don't know why I bother, though. She shouldn't let the illusion of Zane falling in love with her get into her head, because that's never going to happen. Men like Zane don't fall for girls who give in too soon. Zane loves mystery and more than that, he goes after what he can't get.

Such as Lindsay.

Although he had her once, she still manages to keep the upper hand. She's playing the game just like a man. Have sex and never call back or expect anything further than that. Now that's a fresh breath of air, even intimidating. And, I'm almost sure Zane is wondering if he did something wrong to elicit that kind of reaction from her. Maybe the sex was mediocre, wasn't hard enough, or too hard, or he didn't work enough to make her reach orgasm, or came too early or too late. All those doubts and more must be eating at him for not being able to turn Lindsay into one of those girls who revere the ground he walks on.

"I know what you're thinking." Zane's date finally opens her mouth to speak, and she has actually a nice, sexy voice. "I'm wasting him."

I shrug. Sometimes it's better not to talk. Especially when conveying hurtful thoughts.

"I wish I could convince my heart to stop beating for him. Every time I take the plunge and decide to move on, he shows up with the most exquisite gift, telling me I'm the woman he wants for the rest of his life and then just like that he wins me back again."

So she's aware she's being manipulated, yet can't put an end to it. "I'll share a secret with you, and hopefully you'll keep it between us."

She nods eagerly, perhaps expecting me to reveal the key to Zane's heart or something as valuable to gain his love. But that's not going to happen. "You're not the only woman he's using. He has two assistants whose only job is to deal with the women in his life. It's not only three or five women I'm talking about. He has hundreds of women whom he's keeping on the side. If I were you, I'd run from him. He'll come after you, but not because he loves you or cares about you, but because he doesn't want to lose his toy. I'm sorry to be so blatant, but I believe you deserve the truth."

Her gaze drops down to the champagne glass in her hand, and I see a drop of tear rolling down on the side of her nose. "Thank you for your honesty," she says, pulling the sapphire ring from her middle finger, and placing it on the table before vanishing into the crowd of people.

Zane will be pissed off when he realizes he's lost one of his admirers, and I'd pay money to see his face then. I risk a glance toward Lindsay's table and see her in a deep conversation with Zane. Why doesn't she tell him to fuck off? Does she care about him? Zane is one step ahead because of his impatience and disobedience. As his brother, Lindsay won't give me a second chance. That's far from a fair game.

Chloe and Dylan return to the table and Michael joins us while the deserts are served. He talks shamelessly and loudly about married life and secrets behind a happy marriage, as if he hadn't pushed my mother to kill herself.

Soon our table is surrounded by people who want a glimpse into Michael's world as a husband.

Despite the heavy knot in my stomach, I stay and listen to his bullshit. Mom received nothing but suffering for loving the wrong man, and Michael's late-bloomed homosexuality was only a part of her life-long depression and grief. He wouldn't let her go even though he took a male lover. She lived a torturous life filled with physical and emotional abuse. Only we, her children, knew death gave her the freedom and peace she could never have with Michael.

Even so, I can't control my egoist side and wish she was alive, supporting us through the hardness of life that came with being Michael's children. Michael should have been the one to die in place of Mom. This engagement party would be so much different with her.

I keep up my fake interest, while Michael's preaching takes a new turn toward business and politics and steal glimpses, every now and then, at Lindsay. Zane has occupied her time for longer than normal, and I wonder why Michael doesn't intervene. When I see Lindsay laughing at something Zane says, I can't hold it together. I apologize politely, and after Michael's brief nod as his permission for me to leave, I head to the restroom.

I shouldn't care so much about a woman, much less someone under Michael's contract, but I do, and so help me if I let her go without a fight. I keep myself busy checking my emails on my phone while waiting at the end of the hall where the restrooms are located. Lindsay hasn't used the restrooms yet. Which means she'll have to come here soon.

After half an hour of losing time with reading unnecessary emails, I smile at the correctness of my prediction and nod at Lindsay as she enters the restroom. I'm glad Zane doesn't accompany her. He has never been a gentleman.

When she leaves the restroom, I gesture to her with my chin toward an empty room across from the restrooms, and grin when I realize she's put on makeup. Her lips are a glowing crimson, her cheeks a tantalizing hue of pink. Her hair is brushed into thicker volume, wilder waves. And all I can think about is smearing that lipstick around her lips with a hard kiss, deepening the pink of her cheeks, messing up her hair as I take her ruthlessly over the sofa before the windows.

This might be the only chance I get to convince her to give me a shot at pleasuring her, and I won't screw it up by talking bad about Zane.

"I have a secret to share with you."

She lifts her eyebrow with curiosity and takes a step toward me. An aura of lust fills the air as I recognize the craving of intimacy in her expression. I let my eyes sweep over her body, slowly and deliberately to give her a glimpse of the lustful thoughts running rampant in my mind. Her chest grows wide with a deep breath of air and she stops short in the middle of the room, leaving a safe distance between us. "It won't be a secret if you share it."

Her words pull out an unexpected grin out of me. "You're right, but I'll do it anyway."

"Okay, I'm all ears."

And I'm all cock when I'm around you. "The reason you won't consider me as a lover at PE is because I'm Zane's brother and you had sex with him. Am I right?"

She doesn't blink an eye or move an inch when she says, "yes."

"What if I tell you Zane and I aren't biological brothers? Would you reconsider your decision?"

The frowning conquers her face again, this time deeper and harder. "What do you mean?"

"I mean I'm adopted. My biological mother and father are different from Zane's. I have no genetic connection to Zane. I'm no different than any other man to Zane in terms of heredity."

She takes a moment to analyze my confession. Perhaps she still won't back down from her decision because Zane and I are raised as brothers, shared the same household, and grew up under the same rules. "Is that true?"

"Absolutely. Around the time I was conceived, a journalist managed to find out the truth about Michael's sexual tendencies. To prove him wrong and repair his public image, Michael decided to buy me from my birth mother and showed me as his and Mom's third biological child. Mom played along, even had pictures taken of her fresh out of the hospital after her phony birth. Everybody believed the happy and loving family Michael had and still has, and the journalist who originally discovered the truth about my father's homosexuality was arrested and put in jail for spreading false rumors about him."

"That's... That's..." She covers her mouth, looking disgusted as if she'll puke. "That's repugnant. So much dishonesty and fraud. Is there anyone who's not involved in lies in your family?"

She spins around on her heel and storms toward the door.

I run to block her way before she can open the door. "I am. I don't deceive people. I do only what I have to not to get on Michael's wrong side, but that's minimal."

She yanks my hand away with such force I tremble, and moves away toward the window, holding the place that I held on to her arm. "Why is everyone talking as if Michael is the devil on earth?"

"I hope you won't have to experience that side of him, but he'd beat the devil himself in evilness. But that's not the point. The point is, you and I have an unfinished business, and there's nothing immoral that stands in our way to complete what we've started."

"There's nothing immoral for paying money to have sex?"

"Not when the man is willing and would do it without getting paid. All my men are well off and would do it without money. Money is just icing on the cake, but the cake is the real incentive in my business, not the icing."

"The age-old discussion again. Okay, okay, I

understand your perspective and well, you might be right. But, I'm not sure if I'll choose you as the extra escort you offered me." She stares down at her nails then looks up at me. Frown and worry lines cross her forehead. "Zane and you might not have a biological bond, but you're still brothers in heart."

"Believe me, that can't be farther from the truth. He and I despise each other like deadly enemies. Actually, I'm pretty sure he's coming after you because he's aware of my special interest in you."

Her features soften with an unexpected grin of her beautiful lips, and she averts her gaze in embarrassment.

"What is it?" I ask, curious about what might change her angry attitude.

"I didn't know about your special interest in me."

Oh, that. "Even a blind person could see it, how can't you?"

"Is that why you chose yourself to apply the coconut oil to me?"

"I'm only a man. I lose my limits when it comes to taking advantage of a situation to devour a sexy girl."

"You gave me four on the beauty scale, remember? Now you're talking about my irresistible sexiness."

"Well, I admit I was a bit harsh in my judgment of your looks."

She grazes her lower lip with her teeth and cocks her head to the side, her eyes traveling up and down my body. "So you're saying you don't think I'm a four?"

I shake my head no.

"Then which number would you give me?"

"Numbers don't matter in your case because there's no number that can objectively rate my desire for you. The quickening of my blood every time you shoot me a seductive glance, when you bite your lips, run your fingers over your neck as if you want to be kissed there, and when you can't even hide your own arousal. You're sex on legs, Lindsay, but also a fool for not being aware of your effect on men. I had to give a four for your looks to prevent my men going vandal to get you."

"Now you're exaggerating," she says, but the full-tooth smile revitalizing her face tells a completely different story.

I move closer to her and trail the tip of my index finger down her bare arm, feeling the goose bumps along the way, watching her lose control. "You can't even imagine the things I want to do to you."

"Enough." She breathes in and out through her mouth. Her body shivers visibly under my touch.

"Enough or I won't be able to control myself and let you take me here?"

She gasps and then presses her lips tightly together, perhaps to stifle a moan. I wish she moaned and let her words of her lust for me come out of her mouth. But instead she says, "enough, or I will slap you to end this little seduction game of yours. You blame Zane for going after me as a reason to make you upset, but I think you're guilty of the same crime. Would you still have cared about me if Zane hadn't been in the picture? No, don't answer that." She lifts her hand and holds it before my face. "I know the answer. You pulled your coconut-oil trick on me, knowing it was Zane who was waiting for me, and now you have the nerve to blame Zane for your own mistake," she says and paces out, banging the door closed behind her.

I plop myself on the couch and gather my head between my hands, letting out an angry, exasperated breath. No matter what I confess or do, she won't bend. She's uncompromising, close-minded, and stubborn as a mule, and I wish more than anything to weaken her determination for my own indulgence.

The Offer

Hawkins men are something to marvel about, even Ace, who claims to not belong to the Hawkins family.

They're all experts in impressing everyone around them with their charisma and intelligence, and don't forget their exquisite looks. They're all driven in whatever area they choose to excel. One common area all three are good at is seducing women. Even Michael, though he has no interest in the female gender, will spare an extra enticing glance to cause us shaky legs. And, the last of all, they won't give in until they get what they desire.

Take Ace. He wants me, desires me to the level of sharing a nasty family secret with me so I allow him to be my second lover in a threesome. Unless I do a paternity test, I have no way to prove the truthfulness of his words, but the pale blondness of his hair as opposed to the darker tones of his siblings and father tells me he might not be lying.

I don't know what to think, let alone decide if I want him. Well, I actually know that I want him. With all my cells and fibers, with my dreams and realities. I yearn for him. I crave his touch. I melt for his kiss. As if those weren't enough, I'm constantly thinking about him, so much so that if I give in to my needs for a second when I'm with him, I'll find myself on my knees, begging for him to complete that unfinished business.

I want to see him naked in front of me, both his body and soul. I want him exposed, without any barrier or hindrance to conceal his true self from me. I want to get to know his vulnerabilities and capabilities. I want to tire him with my demands and become exhausted with his in return. I want a fight with him, sweaty and painful, and then love him gently to smooth his pain. I want him to belong to me completely with everything he has, even if it'll be for only a brief moment.

Nothing or no one else should matter at that moment. Whatever it is that I'll share with him; I want it to be irreplaceable, incomparable in his eyes. I want a large part of his memory dedicated to me long after I'm gone.

That is, if I decide to have that moment with him.

But if I go ahead and choose him as the complimentary lover, none of this will happen. We won't be able to completely give ourselves to each other in the presence of another man. Perhaps it's not a bad thing after all. If I get lucky and experience the moment of my dreams with Ace, most likely that'll be the last day my heart will belong to me.

I'm not ready to fall in love, much less with a Hawkins. Much less with someone who runs a brothel and has an easy access to hundreds of willing women who won't shy away from shelling out thousands of dollars for his able hands. And definitely not with a man like Ace who doesn't need a brothel to find women.

He's like a perfect poem, words rhyming seamlessly with each other, but their real beauty comes from the meaning that gives life to them. His eyes, the way he looks right through my core and the way his words reflect his own tortured soul are my undoing. It's obvious... if I ever get a taste of his sexual side, I'll never truly be able to let it go and be my normal self again.

I will say no to his offer. I'll pick JJ and another man who have no motives beyond satisfying me while getting their own gratification and that will be it. No hearts will be broken; no tears will be shed.

After the party, Edric reminds me to save a date for another shopping spree with him to buy gowns for the upcoming events I'll be attending as Michael's date. He'll be having an important guest from Russia in less than two weeks. I guess Chloe and I will be responsible for entertaining his wife during their three-day visit. Which means more shopping is in my near future.

Before I leave, Michael thanks me for the perfect date—his words, not mine.

I glance back at the crowd to locate Ace, but

he's nowhere to be seen. A part of me—okay a big part of me—hopes he won't be deterred by my rebuff. I spot Zane and grin at his obvious ogling over me.

Perhaps I should choose Zane and Ace to check out what they have to offer. The thought of them both naked fighting for my attention gives me shivers. Rather than giving me pleasure, though, they'll most likely busy themselves with punches and kicks. From what Ace told me, they don't seem to get along in their normal lives; a little competition in bed might turn their dislike into hatred in a matter of minutes. I'd rather continue having them only in my dreams to keep myself from an accidental punch in the face.

I drive back home with Taylor and Adam. Taylor dozes off on Adam's shoulder, and I stare out to the road, considering Ace's offer. To say his offer inflamed wild lust in me is an understatement, really. If Taylor and Adam weren't in the limousine with me, I'd finger myself to cool down the needy nerves inside me, most likely dreaming about how Ace's finger shook them awake with a brief touch, and Zane's abrupt visit to my apartment to fuck my brains out.

The two men together would make a mind-blowing sexual experience. I could suck off Ace's penis while Zane fucks me from behind. Both men losing themselves while connected to me. The thought of it is so wild and arousing and so much better than any of my fantasies, I feel I'm ready to burn in the aftermath of it.

Oh shit, it seems I don't need to wait until after a threesome with them to burn, because my sex is hot like burning coals, clenching with urgency and spreading the heat throughout my body. I turn my face to the side to hide my blushing. I'll have to use my biggest dildo to take edge off, while dreaming it's one of the Hawkins brothers.

The ride feels like hours instead of only forty minutes, and I climb the stairs in my apartment building two at a time to finally get inside my condo and attack my pleasure chest. Grabbing the eight-inch dildo, I smear a generous amount of lube around it and shove it inside me, still standing and fully clothed.

I close my eyes, and immediately the naked images of Ace and Zane appear in front of my eyes, both of their cocks in their full sizes, pointing at me. Ace would approach me first, giving me a full-blown kiss, while his hands played with my vagina.

Zane would spread his arms around me from behind, his cock pressed against my buttocks. I don't know if it'd be possible to take them both inside my vagina, but in my fantasy it seems to be a reality. They'd throw me onto a bed and thrust their cocks inside me, stretching me like I've never been. I'd be surrounded by two beautiful bodies, filled to the brim by two fat cocks.

Plunging the dildo with harder strokes, I fall face-first over the bed and cry out as the tension inside me reaches to its highest. Wild convulsions follow. I continue thrusting the dildo until the spasms die out and pull it out slowly. Its strong latex smell hits my nostrils and I wince. It's nowhere near arousing like a real cock smeared in my juices. If it was Ace's cock, or Zane's, I'd lick it clean, something I've never done with my previous lovers. But, both Ace and Zane are so sexy, I'd demand to do it without them having to ask me for it.

I slip out of my gown and sneak under the bed covers naked. I'll have to take up Ace's offer much sooner than I thought.

The next days until Friday fly in a blur with mundane work activities, except for the exhausting evening of gown shopping. I buy twelve dresses, twenty pairs of shoes, three coats, and several pairs of underwear. Not to mention new make-up and fragrances. The only problem I have to tackle is space, since my tiny apartment has very limited storage.

On Friday morning, I call Ace's office number to inform him about my decision. He sounds relieved to hear from me.

"I was thinking," I say hesitantly. He'll most likely decline my request, but at least I'll have tried. "I'd very much like to try out the threesome offer."

"I'm glad to hear that. I have a hunch that you'll go with two men, rather than a man and a woman."

"You got that right." Why would I pay for another woman's pleasure?

"Have you any experience with two men at the same time?"

"Ahh, no." If you don't count fantasies.

"You can check out our database to decide with whom you want to have threesome with. All of my men have experience in threesomes and orgies; it's part of their training. So, don't worry about having a mismatch. They'll all have your satisfaction at heart, and if you don't feel comfortable and decide to proceed with only one of your lovers, that's just fine, too."

He's seriously thinking I'll pick him and another escort that I don't know, but the other guy will lose the competition and I'll just want to stay with him. I grin, hoping he'll not feel it through the phone. "I'd like to talk to you in person about something personal before going ahead with the selection. Do you have a few minutes for me today?"

"Sure."

"Okay, I'll be at your office in the afternoon?"

"You don't need to drive all the way. Would you like to have lunch together in Westwood? I know a great Italian restaurant."

"Okay," I say hesitantly, hoping he doesn't mean it as a date.

"Say twelve? I'll text you the address."

Smiling to myself, I disconnect and wait for the text. My phone rings with a new text message and I hurry to read it. It just has the address; no additional words of innuendo, not even a "see you" is added at the end. Disappointing.

I hurry to have shower but primp myself slowly and with care. By the end of my grooming, my hair is all flat, my eyelashes double their length and thickness, and my lips dark crimson. I'll have to make it hard for him to resist my proposal, yet I don't want to appear as a hooker and be photographed with him. So, I go for a low-cut red blouse, a pair of black skinny jeans, and black high heels to make my rear stick out.

I drive my new Audi to the restaurant, both excited and nervous at the same time. A few people take notice of me, but don't dare bother me, I guess, for the fear of pissing me off.

I enter the restaurant hesitantly, glancing around to locate Ace, am greeted by a girl at the reception desk. As soon as I tell her I'm with Ace Hawkins, she escorts me to a secluded part at the back of the restaurant and nods as she leaves me alone with Ace.

Ace stands to shake my hand and gets my chair. I take my seat, highly incapable of suppressing the electrifying effect of his skin on mine, and examine him from head to toe. He's wearing a light-blue, button-down shirt with the first two buttons undone and black slacks that flatters his round ass, which makes me want to dry hump him right now. I remember in shame my purpose for putting on tight jeans and high heels to draw more attention to my own ass, because honestly, no matter how hard I try, his is much more eye-catching than mine, and he doesn't even need to try hard.

Placing the cloth napkin on his lap, he regards me with caution and a hint of lust. "I'm glad I get to see you today."

"The pleasure is mine," I reply, stressing on the word pleasure in a suggestive tone, feeling a little slutty and lightheaded.

The corner of his mouth twitches up and he eyes my upper body slowly, without hiding his intention. "I've already ordered for us, as I have only half an hour. I hope you don't mind."

"No, not at all. I like surprises."

"I'm glad you do. So," he says, his eyes on my face this time as he clasps his hands together on the table. "What is it that you wanted to talk about in person?"

I shift in my chair, unsure of how I should start. "It's about you and your adoption."

"Oh." There's a clear discontent in his voice and expression. Was he expecting me to talk about sex? Most likely.

"Yeah. I'd like to ask a few questions if I may."

"I'm not sure if I can answer all your questions, but I promise I'll try."

"Sounds fair. Do you know anything about your birth mother?"

He nods his head a few times, looking ahead beside me, perhaps remembering a distant memory. I have no idea how old he was when he was adopted, or if he has recollections of his birth mother at all.

"She was a Russian graduate student at the Physics department at UCLA, fell pregnant after a rape incident, and wanted to abort me. Around that time, Michael had the problem with the journalist spreading rumors about his homosexuality. Irene, my adopted mother, couldn't get pregnant anymore, or they'd have tried for another baby to show everyone what a happy family and marriage they had. They didn't want to adopt through an agency either as it would have been hard to show the adopted child as their own biological child."

"So," he continues. "Michael decided to

directly pick a girl who wanted to get rid of her child, and my biological mother was the lucky one. She agreed to give me to them in exchange for a big sum of money. Afterwards, she finished her PhD and went back to Russia. As far as I know, she's a renowned professor at University of St. Petersburg. I guess much of the start-up funding for her research project came from the money she received from Michael for her silence."

"You know her actually?"

He separates his hands to pick up his phone on the table and types something on it before handing it to me. "I haven't met her in person. I found out her name when I was fifteen. Fortunately, she's relatively famous so I could look her up. Read her Wikipedia page. Her name is Alexa Averin."

If I had any doubts about Ace's revelation, they all disappear abruptly as I look at the older, female version of Ace with the same hue of blond hair and the exact set of ice blue eyes staring back at me. She has dozens of academic accomplishments, is a devoted advocate for providing equal education rights to children in poverty, but isn't married or has no recorded children. Does she know anything about Ace? Does she wonder what has become of him?

I glance up and see Ace's softened expression. The usual impassiveness has left its place to warmth and a little sadness, and I stare at him intently and with marvel as if I've seen him for the first time. In a way, it's the first time, since he's never been this open to me. I extend my hand to give him the phone, but as I drop it in his hand, I can't find it in me to end the physical contact and lace my fingers through his.

He lets out a sigh, lowering his eyes on our attached hands. "I know what you think, and no, I don't feel any resentment toward her for almost having me aborted or giving me away. She was raped. What would she do with the product of a rape?"

I wasn't thinking about that, but I don't correct him about his wrong assumption of my thoughts. I caress the back of his hand with my thumb, enjoying the softness of his skin. He melts like a kitten being caressed and closes his eyes.

"Sometimes," he says, opening his eyes. "I wonder to myself if I have any aggressive tendencies toward women. I researched a lot about aggression and rape and whether they're hereditary to see if there's a possibility for me to become like the monster who raped my biological mother. The results I found are very confusing. Some state aggression is genetic, others defend that it's a result of the upbringing. I don't know which one to believe. I check myself and my emotions regularly. I watch my words while talking to a woman more than an ordinary man would. Thanks to my work, I've seen every kind of sex that can exist between a consenting couple, and I couldn't for the life of me understand how a man can force a woman to have sex rather than having the chance to watch her moan and shake with the ecstasy of sexual pleasure."

The pained look on his face breaks my heart and makes me want to smooth those worry lines creasing his face. I shake my head and squeeze his hand, letting the phone in his palm slide onto the table in the process. "I don't see a rapist in you. In fact, I feel comfortable enough with you that I'd sleep naked in a bed with you and know you wouldn't do anything I wouldn't agree to."

"Is that why you yanked my hand away when I was massaging you?"

I don't reply as I'm not sure how to categorize that behavior of him while he shoved his finger into me without my permission. I must admit, though, the line he crossed was a vague one. He might have thought I'd given my okay on getting massaged inside my vagina as well.

His finger inside me.

That's not the visualization I need right now, as I'm already soaking wet beneath my panties.

"I believed that the studies that supported heredity as the reason were wrong," he continues once he sees he won't coax an answer out of me. "I convinced myself that I didn't inherit the wickedness of my biological fathe,r and I'd never even dream about raping. Until you came to my life," he says and moves his hand to grip mine in a hard squeeze. "You're my nightmare come true. You ruined all my beliefs about my good nature."

"What are you talking about?" I blink several times, shocked at the new direction of our intimate talk.

"For the first time in my existence, I started fantasizing about forcing a woman into sex. You … You turned me into a crazy mess. I can't control my thoughts or my physical reactions around you. I'm afraid to be alone with you for attempting to do a wrong move that I'll regret for the rest of my life, but I can't help it. My mental faculties take a break and I'm constantly hard when you show up. I can't stop fantasizing about taking you hard."

I should get mad at his words, or better yet, get him familiarized with my iron slap, but instead I sigh loudly, wondering if he's hard for me at this very moment, too, enjoying the thought of him fucking me forcefully. Just like his, my own brain seems to have stopped working, I guess. "How does that fantasy play out?" I manage to ask in my hazed and lustful state.

"Seriously? You want to hear my rape fantasy?"

My arousal overcomes my shame, and I nod with curiosity.

Unfortunately, the server arrives with our plates, interrupting our arousing conversation, and takes her sweet time placing them in front of us, grating cheese on the raviolis and then finally leaves us alone.

Ace pulls his hand away to get his fork and fishes a piece of ravioli out. I mirror his behavior just to appear less interested, but in reality, I'm dying to hear his fantasy. I think I've never listened to a man confessing his dirty thoughts about me. Oh, I've heard a lot of men's fantasies.

Only, they were about some Hollywood celebrities or porn stars. One was about a fictional character in a space opera. But none about me.

Ace takes his glass of white wine and sips unhurriedly, eyeing me with intent. If he's planning to torture me with his silence, he's succeeding it.

"Your fantasy?" I point out, intrigued and upset for him taking so long and making me look impatient.

He places the glass back on the table ever so slowly, glancing at me with dubious eyes, as if weighing his options or trying to get over some kind of internal struggle. "First, I need you to promise me you won't run for the hills. I can assure you, I'll do anything and everything under my control to not make this fantasy come true."

"Okay. Let's hear it." And please hurry!

"It always starts out with me spotting you leaving a club, wearing a mini skirt and high heels. Your ass is my favorite part of your body, and I like imagining it wrapped around by a mini skirt."

Huh! I knew he had a thing for my ass.

"You walk very slowly thanks to your high heels, and I follow you until you're on a deserted street and then pull you onto another small street. I flip you and push you against the wall. You scream but there's no one around to answer your call for help. I reach down between your legs and rip your panties off. The rest is just pure fucking until you pass out."

I squeeze the fork in my hand hard, feeling the cold metal digging into my skin. His eyes are narrowed and burning like fire, as if belonging to another man, not the impassive and controlled Ace who runs a brothel or the hurtful Ace whose birth mother abandoned him. This new Ace is wild and primitive and frankly gives me shivers of fear.

"That'll never happen," I say in an attempt to hide my fright.

"I know. I'll never allow it."

"I'm not talking about that. It'll not happen the way you fantasize it, because I'll not go down without a fight."

"That makes it all the more exciting. The more you try to fight against me, the bigger my reward will be and the harder I'll fuck you."

I gasp involuntarily. "Oh, shut up." I throw him the cloth napkin and it lands on the top of his head. With the fear that's surrounding my heart, I start laughing like a nervous wreck. I relax a bit when he laughs too and the savage expression is erased from his face. He pulls the napkin from his head, folds it, and places it next to my plate,

"I have to repeat it; that's a fantasy only, and I'll make sure it'll never happen, even if it means I'll stop seeing you to protect you."

"Is that fantasy a result of the assumption that I won't willingly have sex with you?"

"Possibly."

"I don't think you have a nasty bone in you. For one thing, a lot of good men and women fantasize about rape. And for another, you run a brothel to ensure women get sexual pleasure. If that's not one hundred percent against the notion of raping, then I don't know what is. If you're honest about your constant examination of your behavior, even in the heat of blinding lust, your rationale will kick in and prevent you from making a mistake."

"I hope your assumptions are true. I really hope that, because I don't want to hurt you or any other person for that matter."

We eat our raviolis and drink our wine in silence. After the waitress brings us our desert and leaves, I clear my throat to mentally prepare myself for my indecent proposal. "I wanted to talk to you about something else." I bite my lip, hesitant to go on.

"Sure," he says when my pause takes too long.

"I kinda decided who I want to have threesome with."

He raises an eyebrow, a trace of a smile grazing his lips. "Oh, yeah? Who are the lucky winners?"

"One is you."

His smile broadens with amusement, and he leans back against his chair, the move making his shoulders appear twice their size. "And, the other?"

"Zane." I watch the smile freeze on his face, and he resumes his old deadpan, controlled expression that chills my heart in an instant.

"That's not gonna happen."

"Why? Because he's your adopted brother?"

"No. It's not that. I can't stand the thought of being with him in the same room, and you want me to share a woman with him? It'll likely end up in a bloody fight rather than a pleasant memory to remember."

"Oh. That wasn't how I pictured it," I say, disappointed, although that's what I feared might happen.

"You actually fantasized about it?" His tone is accusatory and hurtful, as if he hasn't just told me about his raping fantasy.

If he wants to disguise himself behind his cold mask, I'll have the up most pleasure to play mean. I frown and shoot him a glare. "And masturbated on it, too."

"You really like him, don't you?" His face is still cold and controlled, but there's disappointment coating his voice.

"No, I don't. I don't like you, either." I'm angry, and I sound harsh, but that's okay. I'm not the one to hide feelings, especially when angry. "It's only sex. Nothing else. Why are you acting like a whiny teenager all of a sudden? He works for you as an escort. You offered me a complimentary man for a threesome, including yourself. I enjoyed both occasions I had with you and Zane, and now I want to have you together. That's not against the rules, but you're coming up with irrelevant emotional problems. This is your business. Get over your emotional issues and do your job"

"You're right. There's nothing against the rules in theory, but we're talking about Zane and me here. Zane and I don't get along at all. There have been more than a couple of times that we ended up hurting each other physically. He doesn't like me and I don't like him. There needs to be at least neutral feelings among the parties for a threesome to be enjoyable. In this combination, I can assure you that you won't enjoy it in the least."

"If that's the case, why did you hire him as an escort? Why do you allow him anywhere near your clients and employees?"

"Fair question with a simple answer. Michael. He told me to hire him. I'd declined Zane's application twice. When he couldn't get what he wanted, he complained to his Daddy, and once Michael asked me to hire Zane, I couldn't say no."

"Why? I thought the company was fully under your proprietorship."

"Why?" He raises an eyebrow. "Don't talk as if you don't know Michael. The company might belong to me, but I don't have the power to refuse his orders. Nobody can say no to him, not even his children."

"Now you're throwing mud at an additional person."

A pained smile spreads across his face, not really reaching his eyes. He drops his fork on the table and tosses the napkin beside it. "I'm in no place to tell you what to believe in, but let me at least give you a friendly warning. Michael and Zane are the most dangerous two men you can ever meet in L.A. Please, keep your distance from them. If you ever happen to get into trouble, consider me as a friend. I'll try to help you as much as I can." Standing, he pulls out his wallet and throws a hundred on the table. "I'm sorry I can't stay longer. I have work to do." He leans in to give me a kiss on the cheek, and I let him because I'm taken by surprise, and then watch him leave.

I rest my head between my hands, exhausted and moody for having gone through an intense conversation with Ace. From his birth mother, to a rape fantasy, and then to a dangerous warning about his own father and brother. The talk was everything but what I expected. I see now my wish to have both Zane and Ace devour me will remain as a fantasy forever.

First Zane, now Ace. What is it with Michael's sons and their dislike for him?

I gather my handbag and leave the restaurant. My stomach rises, though I don't think the meal had anything to do with it. I drive to Taylor's apartment to spend the afternoon with them, help them pack for their move to their new home and hopefully help my mind take a break from the Hawkins men.

Taylor fixes us tea and settles beside me on a couch in the living room, while Adam bustles around, gathering items and placing them in large cardboard boxes.

"Adam's older sister is coming tomorrow from New York, that's why we're trying to get everything done by tonight," Taylor whispers when Adam leaves for another room.

"That's an ambitious goal. Do you need my help?"

"If you don't mind?"

"I love to help. What was her name? Adriana?"

"Yeah, the one who doesn't like me. Well, I can't say any of his sisters like me at all, but Adriana really hates me," Taylor adds.

"Pain in the ass."

"You can say that."

"How long is she gonna stay?"

Taylor shakes her head. "She's moving to L.A."

"It'll be fun," I say with sarcasm.

Adam shows up behind the couch and bows to give Taylor a kiss on the forehead. "What are you two whispering about?"

"Your beloved sister and how much she adores me," Taylor says with a mock glare.

"I'll make sure she keeps her claws in," he promises. "I can't wait to see my nephew. He'll turn one in two weeks."

"He's her fourth kid?" I ask.

"Yeah, in eight years," Taylor replies, her face showing a hint of dismay. "And, she still has a great career. I'd ask her how she does it, but I'm afraid she'll bite me if I dare ask her a simple question."

Adam settles between Taylor and me on the couch. I turn to him, elbowing his ribcage, and he jerks away from me. "How can a man as sweet as you have a witch as a sister?"

Adam laughs loudly, doubling over and shaking. "I was thinking the same thing about you as Taylor's witch sister."

"Come on, guys." Taylor gets onto her feet. "Let's finish up with the boxes before three so we can deliver them before the evening. I don't want to hear Adriana complaining nonstop about the unopened boxes."

Taylor assigns me the kitchen, and as I start wrapping the glasses with newspapers, I notice a box with 'baby clothes' written on it. When she leaves, I open the box and see baby clothes with price tags on, folded nicely, with a sonogram picture on top of them. My heart breaks and I feel physical pain as I examine the picture. My poor little niece didn't get a chance to wear the clothes her parents had bought for her.

Swallowing down the threatening sob in my throat, I place the picture back in the box. As I start to turn, a positive pregnancy test in a Ziploc bag catches my attention.

Right at that moment, Taylor shows up at the doorway, staring at me wild-eyed.

"Is this new?" I ask, holding up the plastic bag in my hand. She paces forward, grabbing the bag from my hold, and hides it carefully under the baby clothes. I repeat my question, this time whispering, and she nods, placing her index finger over her lips, signaling me to keep silent.

Holy fuck! How can she expect me to keep quiet at such superb news? I jump over and hug her tightly, screaming at the same time. She reaches over and covers my mouth with her hand, hushing me with an angry look on her face.

"Why?" I ask with a low voice. "Haven't you talked to Adam yet?"

"No. I'm late only by a few days, but I couldn't wait to get tested. It's too soon to tell it to anyone. I was shocked when I saw it turned positive. It can be a false positive, you know, and even if I'm really pregnant, the risk of having a miscarriage at this point is too big. I'll wait for another week to try another test. Don't mention it to anyone. I'm begging you."

"Okay, okay, I won't. But stop being a Debby Downer for once. Third time's the charm. Oh, my goodness, I can't believe it." I hug her again, careful not to squeeze her too tightly with my arms. Only when we hear Adam's footsteps do I let her go and get back to my assigned chores.

I pack until the evening and then help load the boxes into the brand-new truck Adam bought just for the move. Despite Taylor's request for me to stay for dinner, I excuse myself as being tired, which is true. My muscles feel sore and not in a good way.

"Call me immediately if something unexpected happens," I whisper in her ear but hope at the same time nothing bad will happen, and she'll have a healthy and happy pregnancy. If anyone deserves it, it's Taylor.

I walk back to my tiny, dark condo, warm up some left-over lasagna from last night, and settle with it and my laptop on my bed. I'll have to go through the PE database to pick my lovers for tomorrow's fun.

Given the low rating I received for my looks, I don't have access to the hundreds of escorts like Ace promised, but rather fifteen men who are mostly above thirty five and a little too muscled for my taste. JJ is the only one I can imagine myself with among the list of the fifteen interested. I click on the three-hour option on JJ's profile page for tomorrow afternoon between two and five and enter the company credit card number I was given for my personal purchases.

As for the second lover, I'll have to ask Ace if he's still interested in being the complimentary one. I seriously doubt he will, considering how disappointed he was after hearing my desire to have him and Zane together, and he won't be entirely wrong about his frustration.

What was I thinking? Ace might not be biologically related to Zane, but they grew up together like brothers. Having them together in a sexual act would still count as incest.

I pick up my phone and stare at it hesitatingly, wishing I had the balls to call Ace to ask him if he's still interested. After minutes of internal struggle, I accept being a coward and text him instead.

"I'm sorry for the lunch. I shouldn't have asked you to consider having a threesome with Zane. I hope you'll forgive me. I really want you to be a part of the threesome. I already chose JJ to be the third."

My heart leaps when my phone rings with a new text from Ace.

"Excellent choice. Apology accepted." He really isn't into sexting or is still cross with me.

After dinner, I go through my lingerie

collection to pick something appropriate for tomorrow, but I'm sure it's useless, because I have a feeling that the boys will have their own choices for my clothing.

JJ and Ace. In a way, this combination is better than Zane and Ace because I haven't really had sex with either of them, and now I'll get to have them both at the same time. Just thinking about being naked in front of two hot men, who desire me as much as I desire them, makes my insides melt.

To distract myself and ease my agitated nerves, I log into my Netflix account and fire up the first episode of the last season of Frat House. Even though it's the third time I've watched it, the handsome boys of the show keep me diverted, which again makes me wonder how the Hawkins Media board members can be against such a popular show. They surely must have a lot of money to be blind to the success of it.

The Explosion

If I was agitated yesterday, now I'm perplexed for the impending hours at PE. I couldn't sleep well; consequently my eyes are swollen and have dark circles around. As if that's not enough, I have a pimple on my forehead the size of a pea. My hands are shaking. My chin is trembling. This is worse than how I felt on my very first date with a boy.

Nick opens the door of my Audi and I hand

the key to a shirtless valet before sliding my arm around Nick's. I'm wearing a strapless, red, mini-dress and black high heels. I can hardly make it to Ace's office on shaky legs without incident. Nick smiles at me when he opens Ace's office door for me.

I'm a little taken back when I realize Alexander, the third jury member who rated my appearance on my first day at PE beside JJ and Ace, is sitting at Ace's desk. He gets up, walks around the desk, and grabs my hand to shake. "Hello, Seven, thanks for your visit at Pleasure Extraordinaire today. Ace is getting ready for the afternoon, that's why I'll be serving you for your preparation. Would you like to eat or drink anything?"

"Hi Alexander. No, I'll just go ahead and refresh my makeup."

"Sure. I placed the robe Ace would like you to wear for the party."

A robe? There goes my choice of dress for today. I don't voice my annoyance and go through the door to the attached room, closing it behind me. The robe is a small piece of red, transparent clothing. Analyzing its texture in my hands, I ask myself why I even went through the trouble of picking up a sexy dress. They'll always come up with something sexier and more revealing. At least Ace and I both had the same color in mind.

Sliding out of my dress but keeping my crimson bra and panties on, I shrug on the robe and examine myself through the mirror. I'm sure Ace and JJ wanted me to be fully naked underneath, but no power in the world can make me walk naked—yes naked, because the robe doesn't cover anything—all the way to the suite.

After applying my dark-red lipstick and fluffing my hair over my shoulders, I go back and let Alexander walk me to the suite.

My mouth goes dry once we arrive in front of the door, and I regret not having asked for a glass of water. I sigh heavily and feel my cheeks go hot. I'm sure they're now the color of my lipstick.

"Ready when you are," Alexander says as he holds the doorknob. I nod after inhaling a long, deep breath that should calm me down but does the exact opposite, and swallow hard when the door is opened. "I wish you a great afternoon," Alexander says, gesturing with his long arm inside the suite.

I hesitate to take a step, but force myself to

enter anyway. JJ and Ace are sitting on a sofa at the other end of the suite, both naked from head to toe. Both look up and stand when they notice my presence. As soon as I'm inside and the door is closed behind me, Ace orders me to take everything off, his voice clipped and angry. I narrow my eyes at him, cocking my head back. How dare he speak like that to me.

I take off the robe anyway and drop it on the floor, letting it pool around my legs. I wait for a moment for either of the men to come and help me with the bra and panties, but they don't move an inch, so I help myself out of them, under the intense and curious eyes of the two men.

"Shoes, too," Ace commands, and I do, feeling angrier at his hostile attitude. However, I realize my anxiety is diminishing as anger replaces it. Perhaps Ace is doing it on purpose, to ease my tension and get me in the mood. He's perceptive to know that side of me.

After I'm completely naked, I stroll toward them. My heart is pounding heavily under my chest, in my ears. The two men stand a foot from each other, JJ with a massive hard-on, Ace not affected at all by my nudity. I remember he wasn't hard at that time when he wanted to rub coconut oil on me but instead got aroused as he proceeded. Perhaps he needs some work to get hard in addition to visuals. I don't mind working on his cock and seeing the effect of my hands on him.

JJ winks at me as he takes his cock in his hand and starts rubbing it up and down. He's a pro through and through, and the sight of him teasing himself while gazing at my body with lust makes me wet between my legs.

When I finally stand before them, I have to look up to see their faces because I can barely reach their chest level without my high heels. They're both so hot; I can't believe this is actually happening.

"You're stunning," JJ says with a seductive tone, but doesn't make a move on me and just keeps on staring at my body with seductive fires in eyes. Perhaps he's waiting for me to make the first move, to make sure that I don't start anything without being absolutely ready for it. I give up on that idea when Ace reaches up for my hand, pulls me against his naked, firm body, and wraps his arms around me. JJ was waiting for his boss to start the show, I see.

My skin tingles at the places Ace's hands are touching, while the rest of my body screams to be devoured by his lips. I place my hands on his chest, moving them up and down, grabbing his hard muscles with force. I bet he prefers to be manhandled than massaged gently. He presses his lips together, while scolding me, perhaps in disbelief. Yeah, Mr. Ice, I can be tough, too. His eyes are burning with flames of lust, so unusual for his otherwise icy eyes, and his chest heaves up and down quickly beneath my rough hands.

Before long, he leans down and captures my lips, catching me off-guard. I vaguely remember my rule for not kissing while using the PE men for my sexual pleasure. But that belief seems irrational now that I get a taste of Ace's delectable lips.

I stand up on my toes and move my hands up to wrap them around his neck, enjoying the sweet sensation of my breasts grazing over his skin. He tightens his hold around me, shuddering just like me at the sudden crush of our bodies. His hands easily reach the sides of my breasts, and I'm dying for him to grab them.

I gasp with pleasure. His kiss is possessive and urgent. He's licking my lips, as if he's been hungry for me for a long time, and slips his tongue into my mouth. Opening my mouth wide, I suck his tongue and bite it gently. It's nothing like I've tasted before. Sweet and soft, yet aggressive. This is our first kiss, and in a way, I feel like it's the first kiss of my life.

His cock gains thickness between our bodies. I pant with desire to palm it, feel it pulsating in my hand, and then take it into my mouth, then into my vagina.

I feel hands moving down and touching my butt, and I remember JJ is in the room with us. Ace can make me forget about everything with just one kiss, I guess. JJ's hands ferociously knead my butt cheeks while he rubs his hard-on against my back. The feeling is bewildering, revitalizing. I drag my hands down to Ace's chest to push him away and free myself from his hold. First he hugs me tighter, but when I close my mouth, he loosens his grip, tilts his head back, and stares down at me, frowning. Disbelief and shock dominate his face for a second before he resumes his cold self.

Without losing physical contact to Ace's body, I turn to JJ, my butt now plastered against Ace's hot body. His cock twitches teasingly against my back.

JJ runs his fingers through my hair and pulls me in for a deep kiss. His lips and tongue do everything possible to produce the perfect kiss... technically. But JJ's kiss is nothing compared to Ace's hungry kiss. I shouldn't compare, I think to myself. I should just let my body enjoy the two men as they come.

I'm sandwiched between two incredibly hot men and their hard cocks. Does it get better than that?

JJ's mouth moves down to my chin. He licks my throat, then the area between my breasts, moistening my skin with his warm tongue. I moan and throw my head back at Ace's chest as JJ reaches for my breast and sucks its nipple. My body arches against JJ, while I tilt my head backwards and meet Ace's lustful gaze on top of me. He holds me, while JJ does incredible things with my breasts. I feel delicious, electrical charges running across my belly and close my eyes with the force of an impending orgasm.

Orgasm? How? My vagina is yet to be touched. Can one get an orgasm simply by nipple stimulation? Clearly yes, because my legs start jerking as something explodes deep inside me, and I let myself go, dropping all my weight to Ace's able hands.

Before leaving me time to register what's just

happened, both men pull me up onto my feet and change places so Ace is in front of me.

Not taking his eyes off of mine, Ace drops down on his knees and in a swift movement, he drapes one of my legs over his shoulder, his mouth getting dangerously close to my sex. JJ secures his hands on my hips to keep me in place, and honestly, I'm thankful for him because I don't know how else I can keep standing on my feet while staring at Ace's daring eyes.

Ace sticks out his tongue and runs it around his lips, taking my breath away. His long blond hair, blue eyes, untainted skin... He's so beautiful and sexy, like no man I've ever seen or been with.

I grab JJ's hand on my hip to hold on to it and with the other one I reach down and run my fingers through Ace's hair. He hasn't made his move yet, and I have no idea what he's waiting for. Unsure of what to do, I lean down and lick his lips. He's delicious, sensual.

I'm afraid whatever he'll do to me next, he'll break me permanently. I won't be the same person. I'll lose this game of hearts and get hurt. The realization however does nothing to my impatience to have Ace do whatever he desires with me. I'm his to take advantage of for his own sexual pleasure.

It's wrong. It's the only thing I want.

My heart aches when Ace breaks our kiss and turns his attention to my belly. Placing soft, wet kisses, he moves down to my mound. My breathing quickens, so do my heartbeats. His tongue slides between my lips down there and licks my clit. The wetness of his mouth doubles the pleasure, and I moan and twine my leg tighter around his shoulder to get him deeper. He sees my desperation and begins sucking my clit. I jerk at the sudden assault, enjoying the sensation of his lips around my sensitive flesh. His teeth graze around it, and I moan louder.

Letting my clit go, he sneaks his tongue into my opening and grabs my breasts, squeezing them.

"Tastes amazing, doesn't she?" I hear JJ ask between my ragged breathing.

"Hmm, hmm," Ace purrs into me as he plunges his tongue inside of me, spreading me wide open. I buck my hips and grind against his face, giving him more access to devour me. His tongue is wickedly swirling against my insides, which are now swollen and throbbing with the need to explode. His massage on my breasts roughens as his tongue strikes harder. I don't know how much longer I can hold it, but I never want it to end.

My blood is boiling with lust. My entire body is demanding more, harder, sharper. He moves a hand down and at the same moment pulls out his tongue. I manage to look down at him to see what he's up to and feel sweat dripping down my forehead. Before I know it, my clit is captured between his merciless lips and his finger digs into me. I cry out as the tip of his finger hits my sensitive points deep inside. My eyes remain locked on his. He's staring up at me with an astounded expression. His eyes grow wide. His eyebrows are raised. I feel ashamed, as if a secret part of me is revealed to him.

He trusts his finger mercilessly, his lips rough around my clit. There's no stopping now. No amount of will power can prevent the powerful orgasm taking over my body. The warm sensation that starts deep inside my belly spreads all around my weak torso, wrecking me with its supremacy. My entire body freezes as I let myself go with the orgasm that's overpowering me. I can attest I haven't come this violently before. Just with his tongue and finger, Ace gifted me an orgasm much better than anything else I'd had before.

Just as with every beautiful thing, this too has an end. A lump of sadness forms in my throat. This must be it; the little death the French talk about. I'm dying after reaching the nirvana, experiencing the highest of sensations first hand. The higher I fly, the harder I fall. My body is under shock. My soul is shaking uncontrollably. I can't stop falling.

A strong feeling of remorse fills me in. My heart is hammering painfully beneath my chest with the need to bond. Why? Why can't I enjoy a simple sexual experience with a man without developing feelings for him? What is wrong with me? I'm reckless to let this happen, having known of my weakness for quite some time now.

I saw it coming. I knew sex with Ace wouldn't be just a casual hook-up. The signs were clear; the coconut oil he rubbed me with didn't have any special ingredient in it. It was Ace's hand that magically drove me wild. But, never have I imagined a man was capable of giving me this level of pleasure in its purest form. My body is still trembling with the aftershock of the orgasm. My mind is a blur. My soul yearns to connect and share this unique experience.

With Ace. Fuck!

I'm a lost cause. No joy comes for me without a follow-up sacrifice. I should have gone with JJ from the beginning. His able hands and mouth would have given me a great orgasm, too, and I wouldn't have this uncomfortable guilt of letting someone into the depths of my soul.

"Are you okay?" Ace asks, glancing up at me, still on his knees.

"Yes," I snap and slide my leg down. His gaze is tender, and soft, and makes me feel all the more embarrassed for my neediness. I don't want him to dive deeper into my heart.

I turn to JJ and reach up to kiss him, hoping his kiss will erase the strange feeling swarming over my body and my heart. He cups my buttocks and wraps my legs around him, his hard cock pressing against my opening. "Take me," I whisper to his ear. His kiss grows deeper with my words, and he throws me over to the bed, falling on top of me as I fall.

I close my eyes and savor his kiss, working hard to not compare it with Ace's. I slip my hands through his thick brown hair and press my lips harder against his. After minutes of breathless kissing, he pulls up, snatches a foil package on the bed, tears it open, and quickly rolls it down his long, hard shaft. I moan as he adjusts his cock against my entrance and eases into me.

"Yes!" Make me forget. Make me forget.

JJ smiles down at me and moves to hover over me while driving his cock deeper into me, stretching me. "Jesus, Lindsay, you're so tight."

"And you're very—" My sentence is cut off by a pair of hostile lips taking over my own.

Ace parts my lips forcefully and shoves his tongue into my mouth. His hand cups my chin possessively as his tongue pushes inside and attacks mine. Something has to be said about his vicious tongue. It was inside of me not five minutes ago and still isn't tired enough to give up conquering my body. I moan into his mouth at his unexpected yet delicious attack, surrendering all too quickly.

Ace moves his hand down to my throat, squeezing me but not enough to restrict my breathing. I'm sure he's trying to convey to me his fury for not letting him inside my body. He bites my tongue. Not too painfully, though, just enough to make me flinch with shock. Guiding my tongue into his mouth, he sucks it gently yet possessively.

I quiver and squirm at his wicked ministrations. His hand wanders over my chest and cups my breast, pinching and pulling my nipple. I cry out with the pain of it. He breaks our kiss to tend to my hurting nipple, licking it gently, then mouthing it fully. My body arches toward him, begging him to do the same to every inch of me.

JJ picks up the speed, shaking my body with each trust, growling above me. His thumb is rubbing my clit, while Ace continues his intoxicating treatments with his mouth on my other breast. His tongue swirls around my nipple, teasing it mercilessly. I'm breathless. My entire body is hot and pulsating with raw sensations consuming every inch of my being. I grasp the bed sheet in an effort to get some control back to my body. But it's useless. At this rate and intensity, I'll explode with a much stronger orgasm. It'll be loud and tearful. The feeling is so strong, I'm afraid I'll lose my mind in the process. I groan and bite my lower lips.

All of a sudden, Ace disconnects from my body, taking his warm hands and wet mouth from my oversensitive skin. I swallow hard, glaring at him, feeling abandoned and angry at his startling move. Does he know I'm this close to the explosion of my life? Does he even have the slightest idea of what he's taking away from me?

I blink several times. A part of me has the delusion that he's tired, just taking a break, and will go on showering me with his carnal attention in a few short seconds. He smirks and glares at me with a clear case of "How have you enjoyed my little game" written all over his face. Fuck him for being so selfish and cruel. He owns an entire establishment dedicated to sexual pleasure, yet he's denying it to me.

I breathe heavily through my nostrils. My body continues shaking but this time from anger and frustration. Tearing my eyes away from Ace, I turn back to JJ and lift my hands to pull him in. When his face is close to mine, I reach up and suck his lips. I don't need Ace to climax. JJ is as good as he is, if not better. I shift to roll and push JJ under me. Placing my hands on his chest to support my body while he's lying on his back beneath me, I move up and down his cock with swift moves and watch it fuck my vagina.

JJ's eyes close. He's groaning and breathing heavily. "I'm gonna come soon if you keep up the pace."

He thrusts his hips up, driving his cock deeper into me. I moan, louder than I normally would, just to take revenge on Ace. I know it's silly. I should concentrate only on JJ and his cock throbbing inside me.

Ace steps back from the bed and turns around. I see him pick up a cell phone from the nightstand and hear him speak something into it with a faint voice. Though my body is busy riding JJ, my mind is hyper-alert to Ace. His eyes don't leave me; he's intently watching me getting fucked by JJ.

Seconds later, the door opens, I turn to see a beautiful girl with waist-length and curly red hair and pale-white skin stroll into the suite. She's completely naked, save for the strands of hair covering her breasts, and not a bit ashamed of it. With each step she takes toward Ace, her tall, delicate body moves like that of a dancer. Her eyes brighten up with a sensual smile that's directed to him.

"Hi, boss." Her voice is musical and full of intimacy. Who is she? And, why the fuck is she sliding her hand over Ace's chest down to his abs. Ace's cock is hard and slightly touching her skin.

"Want me to take care of it?" She starts to kneel, but Ace holds her hand up. "Go over to the table and spread your legs."

She nods, turning toward JJ and me briefly. Her smile widens at the sight of JJ. "Looks like I'm late to the fun."

"Hello, babe," JJ responds and lets his eyes sweep her up and down. How dare he? I dig my fingers into JJ's shoulder to deflect his attention back to me. He gets my point immediately and grabs my neck with one hand and smashes his lips into mine. I grind my hips against him, hoping to reset my nerves to the pre-orgasmic state.

"Hmm, you don't need that, boss." I hear the girl speaking. I'm dying to see what they're up to but I'm momentarily stopped by JJ's kiss. When JJ's lips move down to my neck, I use the opportunity and tilt my head toward Ace. He's slipping a condom down on his cock as the girl is petting the places on his chest that I rubbed a few minutes ago.

A sudden wave of sheer jealousy constricts my chest. My heart stops when Ace lifts his hand and runs it on her breasts. I watch them, paralyzed, terrified as their bodies connect through Ace's cock as he slides into her, and the girl moans with delight. Ace kneads her breasts, pulling them, and the girl moves forward, wrapping her long arms around his neck.

I can't look away, although I'm feeling physical pain at the sight of Ace giving pleasure to another woman while he's lost in her. He bends and drops his head on her shoulder, and she squirms, possibly because he's biting her there. His hands move down and cup her ass, pushing her closer to him, and he starts fucking her with a furious speed.

Why doesn't he just grab a knife and stab it into my heart? He doesn't even look at my side; he's completely gone for her.

Is he punishing me for choosing JJ over him? Do I mean something to him? Is that why he's trying to make me feel jealous? Or perhaps it's just a game for him, a little trick to excite his clients. I must say he's excellent at it, whatever it is he's aiming for. A rush of boiling anger that I've known only on the day of my niece's death surfaces to my conscious. My heart feels like it will explode with the power of it. I want to hurt someone, that someone being Ace.

I can't do this. I can't, for the life of, me continue feigning enjoying JJ, while torturing myself with watching Ace screwing another girl. JJ must have noticed the change in my mood and is staring at me with curious eyes.

I lean to his ear and whisper, "I'd like to stop this if you don't mind."

He gets the rest of my untold message and slides out of me. I leave a soft kiss on his cheek to thank him for his understanding and watch him leave. Now I have to decide what to do. I can get the fuck out of PE and out of Ace's life, or stay and fight for what I want, although what I want is bordering on impossible.

As always, I chose what's not good for me. If my brain had any power over me, I'd most likely be living a happier life, yet, here I am, stubbornly inventing new ways to torture myself. I'm the walking definition of masochist for getting on my feet and strolling toward Ace and the girl he's fucking, as if watching them from afar wasn't painful enough.

Even though my heart aches at the sight of someone else having what I desire, I can't deny the extremely arousing sight of their fucking. The girl can't keep her eyes open, while Ace squeezes her body between his strong arms. Her soft squeals are in rhythm with his thrusts, and I wish it was me he was devouring.

Ace doesn't look at me for long moments after JJ is gone. He's staring at the girl, who can't keep her eyes open and her mouth closed. I'd leave them alone, if I was sure it was what Ace wanted, too. The fact that he's ignoring me, at least trying to appear so, is proof enough for me that he's using the girl to get revenge on me.

He's a professional; his clients' needs and interests should precede his feelings. But, instead of showing me the attention I want and paid for, he's choosing to punish me for my own little game. Which goes to show he's acting with his emotions. He's probably cross with me. I smile at the thought and lift my hand to caress his shoulder. His eyes fall closed at the touch, and I notice his pace slows down. Good.

"You're so sexy," I whisper, my lips too close to his skin, and I watch goose bumps form on the area of his arm my breath touches. My lips graze softly on his skin and trail along the contour of thick muscles. He's much taller than I, so I have a long way to go until my lips reach his shoulder.

He's keeping up with his avoiding game. I move my hand up, running it through his hair, and grasp a strand to drag his face down to mine. His eyes snap open, as expected, and he shoots me a stern glare. As if that'll scare me in the least.

Parting my lips, I attack his mouth and kiss him with all the anger boiling in me. He kisses me back and soon it turns into a game of who can hurt the other most. He bites my tongue. I dig my nails into his skin. He places his hand against my buttocks to press me hard against the side of his body until I can't breathe. I tug at his hair harder. He slaps my buttocks. I sneak my arm around the girl's leg to reach down for his balls, cupping them not so gently. But he doesn't let go of the girl, and just for that fact alone, he's winning the hurting game.

Instead of squeezing his balls harder, I begin massaging them, brushing his condom-coated shaft whenever it slides out of the girl's vagina. His kiss softens, deepens, and makes me moan with pleasure. His hand moves up and he wraps his arm around my waist. His thumb draws small circles on the side of my belly. I pull my hand away from his hair, drag it down to his buttocks. Their firmness is marvelous. I want to go down and lick them each until my tongue gets tired. I slide a finger between the cracks of his ass cheeks and begin massaging his opening.

His lips and tongue stops moving, but his hips pick up the speed until he's practically pounding into the girl. Her screams fill the room as she lies flat on her back on the table. I go on massaging, and soon Ace's anus opens up to me. I ease the tip of my finger slowly, tenderly, surely into him. He throws his head back, making soft sounds. His eyes close tightly.

I plaster my lips against his biceps and continue massaging his balls with my other hand. With this much stimulation, he should come with an explosive orgasm. His body stiffens, his hips stopping abruptly, and he groans like a hurt animal. Before I know it, he slides out of the girl, grabs my arm, and hauls me onto the bed. I fall face-first onto the mattress.

"Get out," he screams, I think, to the girl and rips the condom off of his cock, tossing it on the floor. As soon as the girl leaves and closes the door, Ace strides forward, places a knee between my legs on the bed, and presses his palm on the small of my back, pushing me hard against the bed. "What the fuck do you think you are doing?" he yells at me.

I freeze on the spot, can't move even if I dare. I think I've never been this scared in my life. Not even when Macey Williams kidnapped me.

The Revenge - ACE

Tasting Lindsay's climax on my tongue had the same effect of a thousand dollar Martini on my taste buds. Once you taste that exquisiteness, everything else will taste nasty, like cheap wine. I could devour her for hours, never getting tired of her special sweet flavor, intoxicating scent, swollen softness of her flesh, uncontrollable twitches of her body, and her moans. Oh, her moans...

She was like a feast; perfect for my palate and

willingly giving herself to me, yielding to my desire. I saw trust in her eyes. Trust to my capability to make her experience something extraordinary, help her see something she'd never see otherwise. And, when she did and fell apart into my mouth and my finger, I wanted to hold her there, in that position, forever, watching her loose herself to me and with me. The only incentive for me to stop and pull my mouth away from her was to let my cock feel her depths too.

I burned with the desire to fill her insides and stretch her to my size, make her cry with pain and pleasure. I wanted to reach to the highest of the peaks together with her, looking deep into her eyes as she gave herself to me completely.

But, no.

She had to fuck with my mind and choose JJ over me. Why she would do such a thing is beyond anything I've known and seen among women. After years of observing them losing themselves in the arms of their lovers, I thought I gained enough expertise to forecast their next steps.

But, not Lindsay's.

She's the most unpredictable creature who's crossed my way. She's been the root of my sleepless nights and inexplicable headaches since she showed up in my life. And, now she is the cause of the most painful hard-on I've come to experience.

As if seeing JJ fuck her wasn't torturous enough, I had to listen to her moans too. Even being fucked by another man, she looked delectable, arousing. Despite my annoyance, I couldn't stop myself from enjoying her. I kissed her like never before. I savored her lips, her tongue, and then her breasts. I have no doubt her moans got louder because of me. My kisses gave her more pleasure than JJ's cock inside her. Yet, even that obvious fact didn't convince her to dump JJ and take me instead.

So, I had to do what I could to cool off and called Jennifer. Even while a quick hand stroking would have finished me off, I was lucky enough to find a beautiful and willing woman to relish. I closed my eyes and made myself believe that it was Lindsay and not Jennifer who was taking me inside her. It wasn't a difficult mission, because Lindsay's taste was still on my tongue. Her scent was still the only thing my nose could detect. It was her face that I saw in the darkness. My ears could hear only her moans.

Seconds pass. Maybe minutes. Lindsay's moans stop, and I hear whispers, then the door closing. I open my eyes and from the corner of my eye see Lindsay approaching. I feel her fingertips on my arm and her warm breath against my skin. She's teasing me with all her power. Kissing me, whispering to me how sexy I look. Dirty, old tricks. I now see what kind of woman she is. She loves chasing and wants what she can't get. Just like a man. That's why she didn't have me when she could, and now that I'm fucking another woman, she's flying around me, like a bee after a flower.

I let her kiss me, pull my hair, cup my balls, and reciprocate the ferocity of her moves with pleasure.

But not that. I won't allow that.

No one can touch me there, finger my anus. I warned her the first time her finger entered me, but it seems she didn't get it, because she's now thrusting her finger into me like a fucking penis. All I can focus on is the vulnerable part of me being violated. She lets another man fuck her in front of my eyes when it could have been me taking her. But, when I fuck another girl, she deems it appropriate to fuck me in the ass.

Isn't it the very definition of obnoxious?

Anger blinds my eyes, and I taste blood. I feel my ears turn hot. I lose it. My sense flies out of my brain, and all I can feel is revenge filling my lungs. I don't remember the moments of pulling out of Jennifer or how I end up being on the bed and pushing my hand against Lindsay's back. But all I can think of is to make her pay.

"Do you want to know how it feels to be fucked in the ass?" I lean down and scream to her ear. I see her mouth moving, but my mind doesn't register any sound. Only the sound of my ragged breaths. I push her legs apart with my hand and run a finger between her ass cheeks, just like she did to me a few minutes ago. She doesn't resist. She doesn't move when my finger slips into her hole.

No! A small voice screams in my head. I try to ignore it at first and grab my penis. It's throbbing in my hand, more so because of Lindsay's aggressive teases. She's woken the hulk, the monster in me, and now she'll have to pay. I move farther, sliding my finger out of her, and press the head of my cock between her ass cheeks. It's met with the resistance of her tight ass.

No! Another voice yells, and I start hearing

faint sounds. Muffled mumbles of a man. How? "Calm down, now," he whispers to my ear over and over again. Suddenly I find myself in a long-forgotten dream. The room is dark and cold, and large hands hold me in place. I feel small, weak, and vulnerable.

"Calm down. Calm down." Who the hell is speaking? An acute pang of fear squeezes my heart, and I inhale a deep breath.

I shake my head, and just like that the noises vanish and my senses flood back to me. The darkness disappears. I look down in front of me and see Lindsay crying and begging, "No," one after another.

What the fuck? My mind is a blank page. I try to remember the last seconds in vain. My eyes drop to my cock touching her ass and immediately shame fills my heart.

"I'm sorry," I mutter. I can't believe I was about to hurt her. What the fuck came over me? "I'm sorry," I repeat and get on my feet. She rolls on the bed, her face chalk white, and her eyes wide with shock. "I'm sorry." I drop down on my knees and cover my face with my hands. I was a second away from becoming the monster I always feared I'd be. What's wrong with me? Her safety should be my main concern, yet I've become the most dangerous person to her.

Tears wet my hands and sobs shake my body. I cry for what it seems to be forever. I feel Lindsay's hand on my shoulder and another on my head. She's stroking my hair like a mother would do to her child when he's wounded. I feel wounded, for coming close to becoming someone I've always despised.

I take her hands between mine, although I have no right to touch her, and press them against my lips. "I'm a monster," I whisper, tasting her skin. She pulls her hands away and wraps them around my neck, pulling me in against her chest. My tears moisten the smooth skin of her breasts, but she presses me harder against her as if she wants to engrave my face onto her chest.

"I started it," she says, and kisses the top of my head. I don't deserve sympathy. I deserve punishment. She pulls me up onto the bed and hugs me. Our bodies curl into each other's, my head resting on her chest, her legs wrapping around my hips.

I've never felt so safe in my life as I feel right now in Lindsay's embrace. She hums a lullaby that I've never heard of, while I continue to sob. No amount of tears can wash away the filthiness of my soul. Although I tried to deny it for majority of my life, I'm the reincarnation of my biological father. A criminal, a bully, a rapist.

We stay there, without moving for long moments. She doesn't try to change position although I'm sure her arm and leg beneath my body must be sleeping. I shift and take her arm into my hand, gently urging her to roll to the other side so I can spoon her from behind. She gets my cue and moves, wrapping my arms around her chest. I snuggle against her back and cup her breasts like a bra. She pushes her ass against my groin. I move back because if I don't, I will get hard, then who knows what I might do to her.

She pushes herself further back. Of course she'll go for what I try to avoid. Doing the opposite of what I intend has become her trademark.

"Don't," I whisper to her ear as a plea.

Rather than listening to my warning, she reaches back with her hand and grips my hip, pushing me against her, plastering my groin to her ass. The touch of her skin makes my cock stir.

"I want you," she demands. There's no hesitation or doubt in her voice.

"Are you sure?"

She doesn't answer me with words. She just backs her ass into me and grinds my cock into its full length.

"You don't know what you're getting yourself into."

"I'll not try to finger you again and as long as you leave my butthole alone, I'm fine with whatever you do to me."

I run my hands tentatively on her back and arms. She moans. Although I enjoy the feeling of her ass against my cock, I want to see her face if we go all the way. I slither down, kissing her neck, her shoulders, and her back, down to her ass.

I hesitate touching her ass cheeks, but my fears evaporate when she pushes them against my face. I lick each of them with care and devotion, while sneaking my hand between her legs to explore her pussy. She's soaking wet and swallows up my fingers easily, rocking back and forth. I dare bite her skin and push my fingers deeper into her. She cries and buries her face into the pillow. Again, just the opposite of what I want.

Raising her leg, I roll her on her back and spread her legs wide so I can bury my face in her pelvis and start licking her all over. She doesn't let go of the pillow and moans her pleasure into it. Her chest moves quickly up and down. Her nipples are erect, her body shaking. Her pussy is squeezing my fingers and if I'm not wrong she's already coming or very close to it. With one swift move, I get onto my knees, push that pillow away from her face so I can see her, and sit between her legs.

"Are you sure you want it?"

"Yes."

"Say it."

"Yes, I want it." Her hand reaches for my cock, and she circles her delicate fingers around it and pokes the head of it against her entrance. Her mouth falls open as my cock slides into her slowly, carefully. When I'm fully inside her, she stares at me with pleading eyes as if asking me to blow her mind away again. That's exactly what I'm planning to do.

I push her legs up to my chest and over my shoulder, feeling the depths of her pussy wrapping around my cock. She cries and throws her head back.

"Look at me when I'm fucking you." Because I don't want to leave anything to guessing. I want to see everything of her, witness my effect on her first-hand, own her pleasure, and feel the euphoria of our fuck together. As much as I want to take her hard and fast, I also want to enjoy this. I want to give her an unforgettable moment. Not because she's my client, but because she urges that need out of me. The more fulfilled she is, the more satisfied I'll feel. I want to touch the parts of her that no man before me could. I want to see her shudder like it's the first time she's having sex.

Sliding in and out of her with a leisurely speed, I move my hand to let my thumb brush her lips. A low moan escapes her mouth. She's forcing herself to keep her eyes open and staring at me as if she's about to cry.

"Please, I'm so close," she whispers to my finger. I shake my head no. I thrust into her with long and slow strokes. Her moan peaks every time the head of my cock hits her core. I feel a sharp spasm inside her and instantly her body goes stiff. Her eyes grow wide and lose focus. She's coming already.

I lean down and capture her lips, trying to catch her moans of ecstasy and to experience the intensity of her orgasm together with her. She's so entranced she can't reciprocate my kiss and only lets out soft whimpers into my mouth. Did she feel this lost with JJ too? With Zane? God, I wish Zane hadn't touched her. Does she compare me with him?

When her lips pick up the rhythm of mine, I pull away, flip her on her stomach, drag her hips up, and pound into her harder and faster. She tilts her head to the side and tries to smooth her hair away from her face to look at me, all the while moaning. Unlike men, the second time takes shorter for most multi-orgasmic women, and I'm glad Lindsay is one of them, because I want her to break apart as many times as possible without me getting her pussy sore. She's pushing her ass to me, matching my thrusts. I come close to exploding into her when her body freezes and her inside muscles begin to vibrate again.

If I come into her, I want to have her face close to me, have her lips within kissing distance, and looking into her eyes. When her convulsions subside, I turn her around and pull her up against me, so she's sitting on my lap, riding my cock.

"Fuck yourself on me," I whisper to her ear.

After a moment of confusion, she gets my wish, wraps her arms tightly around me and starts grinding her pussy against my cock. I don't move; I want to encourage her to do whatever she wants in order to get off by herself with my cock inside her. It's so arousing, I have to focus so I won't spoil it for her before she's done. Her legs are folded, and her knees are pressing my hips to the level of pain. Her hips are smashing into mine each time she bucks them against me.

Beads of sweat form on her forehead. Her eyes are closed, her teeth firmly clenched on her lower lip. Her skin is flushed with the effort of restraint, and she looks rather like a construction worker with the amount of energy she's using.

"That's right, baby."

She growls and digs her nails into me, bouncing up and down on my cock with a renewed surge of energy. Watching her in her near-delirious state makes it impossible for me to keep myself from the threatening release.

"Oh, God, Ace," she cries and throws her head back. I cup her head and push her into me, capturing her lips while waves of orgasm ripple through her body. I thrust my hips forward and blow my thick, hot load inside her. My cock jerking, her pussy convulsing, we savor each other with long, claiming kisses. I haven't exploded this powerfully in my life. She's a little vixen for fucking my mind like this.

Her arms loosen their hold around me, so do her thighs. I let her go, and she sprawls all over the bed, legs and arms wide spread.

"You. Are. Amazing." I collapse on the bed, next to her. My body feels heavy, like a ton of bricks. Our breathing is loud and ragged, and my mind is still having trouble figuring out what's just happened. The unpredictability of Lindsay, coupled with her crazed sexuality, has shot me to the moon and farther.

If I had the tiniest bit of energy, I'd use it to kiss Lindsay, but for now I have to be content with watching her from the corner of my eye. She's staring at the ceiling, looking shocked and paralyzed, just like me.

What's she thinking? Will she go as soon as she's gained enough energy? I wish she would stay and spend the night with me. She'll worry over the contract, I know. That shitload of document that brought her to me but restricts us from going anything beyond occasional, commercial hook-ups.

She starts to get up, but I'm not ready to let her go yet. With the last drop of energy, I reach for her arm and pull her down. Crawling on the bed, I lie down between her wide-spread legs and gaze at her freshly pied and swollen pussy.

Her voice is weak when she says, "Oh, please. I can't come anymore."

"Just close your eyes and relax. It's simply for my enjoyment." Just like everything else I did with you. I dip my head and lick up all the liquid gushing out of her, spreading the lips of her pussy. My sperm mixed with her juices with a hint of latex. Not a terrible mixture. I'd drink poison without hesitation from her pussy, but I'm glad JJ kept his cock sheathed while inside her.

Lazily, she tosses her legs over my shoulders and wraps them around my head. It's clear she won't let me go without giving her a fifth orgasm. Every time my tongue hits the swollen, pink flesh of her entrance, her body shakes with delicious, little tremors. Shielding her eyes with her arm, she raises her hips and pushes them against my mouth. I respond to her untold wish and drive my tongue into her dripping folds.

"Oh, no. Oh, fuck. I can't take this," she whimpers silently, her chest moving up and down faster with each thrust of my tongue.

I slide my hands to her breasts and tweak her erect nipples with my fingers. She pushes her chest into my palms and covers my hands with hers. We knead and rub her breasts together, and I fear it's bordering on the painful, but she doesn't seem to care and keeps on pressing harder. A new surge of juices begins to flow from her pussy. Her legs squeeze hard around my head; her nails dig into the back of my hands. Her moans echo loudly in my ears. Her body goes limp for several seconds. Although I'm dog-tired and my tongue already feels numb, I keep pushing it into her over and over again until I feel her body relax.

Exhausted doesn't even begin to cover how she looks, but even so, she rolls to her side and drops her feet onto the ground. Why is she hurrying to escape me?

"Why can't you just be a normal woman for once and snuggle up with the man you've just had sex with?" I peek up at her flushed face and disheveled hair.

She stares at me blankly. I guess her brain isn't back to its full-functioning mode yet.

I pat at the space beside me, my eyes begging for her to come back and find her place in my arms. "Please. Cuddle with me, be clingy, push me to talk to you, do anything, but just don't go. It'll make me feel like you think the sex was lousy."

"I thought you wanted me to go."

I roll my eyes at her, smirking. "You seriously think that, after I sucked my spunk out of you?"

"Ahh, you admit that it tastes nasty but still expect women to look eager and aroused while swallowing it up. Aren't men full of bullshit?"

I hold out my hand out to her, smiling at her joke. "But, you looked eager while you swallowed mine."

She glances at my hand suspiciously, then laces her fingers through mine, and lies next to me. "To be honest, I didn't really taste it."

"How?" I frown, throwing my arm around her so she won't have a chance to escape. "But it was in your mouth."

"You shot your release at the back of my throat, and I swallowed it quickly. It didn't reach my taste buds. My dislike for sperm is one of the reasons why I've become good at deep-throating. It's too salty, too gooey. Yuck. Don't get me wrong, I love giving head, but sperm just doesn't agree with my taste buds."

I laugh and press my lips on the top of her head for a kiss. Her honesty knows no bounds. "Somebody has to teach you how to lie."

"Oh, really?" She tilts her head back to gaze at my face, her eyes challenging. "So, you'd prefer it if I told you how delicious your spunk is and that I could drink cups of it rather than the most expensive champagnes, after you've just tasted how repulsive it is. Is that what you really want? Seriously?"

"I don't know, but it sure is more flattering."

"Faking an orgasm not to deflate your ego is flattering too, but I don't think you'd want it."

"I can tell if a woman is faking it."

"No, my dear." She shakes her head eagerly. "You can never tell. Men have egos the size of Jupiter, and you're no exception. If a woman comes up and claims you're the best fuck of her entire life, you'd believe her, eyes closed."

"I bet you are the exact opposite and would just smash my words against me if I told you you're the best fuck of my life."

The shock in her face is palpable. Her eyes grow wide. She starts to open her mouth to speak, but closes it before words can form. I wish I could read her mind.

"The last minutes I shared with you were by far the best of my life. Nothing else could come close to it," I say and kiss her mouth, hoping my lips will resolve her speechlessness. When I pull back, her eyes are staring back at me, intently searching for a clue for my honesty. "You're obsessed with being honest no matter what, but can't even tell a lie from truth."

"Is it... is it the truth? I mean the part about the sex with me," she stutters and bites her lower lip as if regretting what she's said.

I roll her over my chest, feeling the curves of her soft body pressing along my own body, her hair teasing my skin. Running my hands through the thick strands, I position her face right above mine and stare straight into her eyes. "As true as the day is light and the night is dark. I'm in awe of you, Lindsay Doheny, aka Seven. I can't think of anything else but you since the day you came into my life, and you just gave me more reasons to continue my obsession with you by giving yourself to me the way I could never imagine in my wildest dreams."

"Now I'm sure you're lying," she says, but her eyes grow large with... fear? Is she afraid that I might indeed be telling the truth? "How many women did you sleep with for me to be the best fuck of your life? Two? Huh! I simply laid there and did nothing, while you did all the work. How can that be best fuck for anyone, much less for someone like you?"

"Someone like me?"

"Don't make me say it."

"What? Because I run a brothel and have seen practically every Kama Sutra position live?"

"I was going to say someone as hot and sexy as you, but your reason sounds more valid." She winks and gives me a sly grin.

"Why, thank you. I'm not lying and I hope the moments I pleasured you meant something to you, too."

She closes her eyes, exhaling a deep breath, and buries her face in my shoulder. Her eyelashes tickle my skin with each blink of her eyes and from the feel of it, she seems to be having a blink attack.

"Don't hide your face from me." I tilt my head so my mouth is close to her ear. "I understand why you don't want to open up to me but at least let me see you." Staying true to her pattern, she doesn't do what I ask her, so I try another method. "Tell me the other reason why you became great at deep-throating."

My question seems to do the trick, because she lifts her head, props on her elbow, and rests her head against her hand. "My ex-boyfriend couldn't make me orgasm with vaginal sex, but he gave great head and would do it only if I sucked him off to his satisfaction. A dead-on example for 'Practice makes perfect,' I guess."

The thought of her lips around another man's dick isn't something I'd like to ponder right now. Or ever. I run my finger alongside her spine and hips. Her skin erupts in goose bumps at the spots my fingertip wanders over. Now, that's a better sight to focus on.

"Your ex is a jerk."

"Yes, he is. I hadn't realized it until I found out he was screwing my best friend, too. He didn't even ask for forgiveness when I caught them riding each other like wild beasts in our bedroom. I'm glad I'm out of that shit." She presses her lips together, looking away, perhaps remembering the pain of betrayal. "I guess mine is but a wishful thinking."

"What is it?" I frown at her, replaying her

words in my mind to check if I missed something.

"Finding a guy who doesn't lie. I'm afraid it's an extinct species."

I smirk at her, shaking my head. She's right. Even though I hate liars, I'm one of them.

"Ah, also he loved it when I massaged his prostate and probed him in the anus," she adds, lifting an eyebrow cautiously, and I'm immediately filled with shame again for responding to her gesture violently. She was only trying to heighten my pleasure the way she learned it.

I stop my wandering hand and pull it away from her. I don't deserve touching her that way. "Look, there's no excuse for my behavior. To say I'm embarrassed to death doesn't even begin to cover how I feel about what I did. I'm very sorry."

When I move away, she slithers close to me, cupping my face between her hands, and kisses my lips softly. Her eyes are open, following mine, assessing my reactions. I let her kiss me and stare back at her twinkling irises, which are conveying soothing words to my soul. What is it with her and her power to render me shocked with each and every move she pursues? I guess I'll never find out.

She pulls away, but her eyes continue their

hypnotist session on me. "You looked pissed off with me. I feared you'd hurt me." Her voice is barely audible.

"I feared that, too, when I realized what I was about to do."

"Haven't you let anyone else touch you... there?"

I give my head a little shake, trying to remember if any woman even attempted what Lindsay did twice. Nope, no one dared explore my back more than the customary groping of the cheeks.

"You weren't that upset the first time. Was it particularly irritating in front of another woman?"

"I was upset the first time, too, but this afternoon you just seemed to do everything possible to get on my nerves. First choosing JJ over me and then dumping him when I had another woman. It's not how I pictured the afternoon with you. I thought you and I would enjoy each other and JJ would be there just to collect the money. Which of course doesn't justify my angry outburst in any way."

"I'm sorry." She drops her eyes to my lips. "I wish I'd done it the way you pictured it, but I got scared."

I grab her hand that's covering my cheek. "Scared of what?"

"I'd rather not say it."

Has she seen my tendency for aggression even while I hadn't been aware of it? Is that why she was scared of staying alone with me in the same room? Is it related to the contract? Did Michael warn her off of getting involved with me? Whatever it is, I'm afraid if I don't act upon it right now, I'll never be able to get it out of her.

I kiss her palm, inhaling her sweet scent, and then reach for her lips. She opens up her mouth for me easily, wrapping her arms around my neck to get more of me. Her kiss is full of confessions, but I wish I knew what they meant. Sliding her leg between mine, she starts teasing my cock with her thigh and damn me if my body doesn't give her the reaction she's aiming for. My tactic seems to be failing. Instead of getting her open up to me, I'm giving her a chance to escape the interrogation. So I do the only thing I can and pull away.

"Please, I want to hear what scared you so much that you chose to annoy me rather than use me for your ultimate pleasure."

Her expression saddens, and she looks at me with concerned eyes. I can feel something big is coming. I hold my breath, anxiously waiting to know how she'll wreck my world. Again.

"Because... because you seem to be the kind of man to whom I could lose my mind over, easily."

What? Not Michael, not even my aggressive outburst, but a love declaration, or something very close to it? She tried to avoid me because she thinks of me as a man she could fall in love with?

Her face is serious. This is real. Not a joke, but a wave of laughter is threatening to burst from my mouth. I swallow hard to stifle it. What to say? That's exactly my thoughts for you? Or, I've already lost my mind over you, and I don't think it'll ever come back to me? With the level of distrust occupying her thoughts, I'll be giving her more reasons to suspect my honesty.

However, the expectant look dominant in her expression is pressuring me to respond to her revelation. I swallow again, sighing, trying to come up with a smart way to show her how I feel, or at least gain some time. My mind, which I'm always proud of for its practicality, is now failing me. She'll give up, collect her things, and go, never coming back. The thought of her gone and me deserted, pinches at my heart. Why? Why do I feel so anxious and insufficient around her as if she's the only woman left on earth, and if I screw it up, I'll be left without love?

Love? Why the fuck am I thinking about love?

She sighs and rolls down, putting a cautious distance between our naked bodies. Oh, no. She's going. That's it for me.

"Ahh, I am..." What? I'm what? I feel like a little boy caught in front of a broken vase and not able to produce a good excuse for it and not the commanding man who gives consecutive orgasms to any woman available to him.

Her hand travels slowly on the bed, and I feel her fingers on my hip, moving to my cock. "Now I really want to taste your spunk."

Huh? What does one thing have to do with the other? If I knew failure to respond has that effect on her, I'd shut my mouth throughout the afternoon.

She shifts and gets on her knees, walking on all four toward south, deliberately, self-assured, spreading fright and excitement all at once, and settles between my legs. Her body is relaxed. Her hands are poised when she moves them on my thighs toward my genitals.

The cold, calculated expression on her face makes me scared. My cock must have stuck itself inside me for the fear. She inhales deeply, parts her lips, and sticks the tip of her tongue out to moist them, and spreads a hand on my flaccid member. I prop myself up on my elbows to get a better view of the action before me.

She takes her time plotting her next move and eyes me with a shivering smile curling up her lips. Just like a wild beast seconds before latching onto its victim, her whole demeanor changes and she launches down and licks my severely tired cock to its full size in a matter of seconds.

I growl at the effect of her mouth on me. She frees my cock from her mouth for a moment to regard her accomplishment with pride. My cock glisters with her saliva and throbs with the need to have her back. I have to fist my hands to keep them from grabbing her head to prompt her to continue.

She glances at me with a smirk, clearly aware of what's going through my mind, and dips her head to give me just what I want. I hiss between my teeth and throw myself on my back when her moist mouth sheaths my cock, and her tongue swirls around the tip of it. She's so efficient with her lips and tongue I'm afraid I won't last longer than a minute or two tops.

A deep, male voice from the intercom startles us both. It's Alexander. "Ace, sorry for the interruption, but your father is in your office and wants to see you ASAP."

"Michael?" I mumble. Lindsay slides my cock out of her mouth and gazes at me questioningly. "This's the first time he's visited PE. Something must be up," I say.

She quickly gets on her feet and reaches for her bra, panties, and the robe. "My dress is in the room attached to your office, but I don't want to meet with him wearing this." She shows me the transparent robe. She shouldn't meet with anyone wearing that except with me. My cock and I watch Lindsay's ass in dismay when she bends down to slide into her panties. Even though I had more than my fair share of her for the day, the disappointment at not having enough time to let her finish me off is big enough a reason for me to get into a fight with Michael for choosing the worst time ever for giving me a surprise visit.

"I'll make sure Nick gets some clothes for you. Are you leaving now? Stay a little longer. We can have dinner together."

"I really can't. I have plans already for dinner."

My eyebrows lift instantly without my control. What? I've slept with her, not asked for her hand. Why am I suddenly bothered by her possible date with another guy?

"With my sister," she adds, looking amused, probably by the murderous expression on my face.

I'm not sure why she had the need to explain herself, but I can't say I disliked her attitude. At least it'll help me focus on the immediate challenge. What is Michael doing here?

"In that case, I'll see you soon?"

She smiles and nods. I get off the bed and walk toward her while she's approaching me. We meet halfway and embrace each other like long-time lovers.

"I'll call you," I promise but my words don't mean anything. Not as long as she's under contract with Michael.

"Yeah, do that." She peeks up at me, quirking

her lips up, and I can't help but lose myself in that beautiful mouth. I kiss her passionately as if we'll start another love session, and it's only when she pulls away, I remember I have Michael waiting for me. He hates waiting like the plague. And worse, he'll likely ask me what took me so long, and I'll have to come up with a lie.

"Don't tell Michael anything about me and you," I say.

"I won't."

I call Nick and order clothes for Lindsay, while trying to put on my pants and shirt. Nick accompanies Lindsay out, and I hurry to my office.

Despite my fear of finding Michael in a rage, yelling at my staff to get me to him dead or alive from wherever I am, I find him chatting and laughing with JJ. I haven't been so grateful for having JJ on my team during his three-year contract with me as I am now. He's superior when it comes to charming people, no matter what the gender is.

Michael is sitting in my chair, behind my desk, as if he owns the office. Although I started up the business with my own money and hard work, he feels entitled to treat my establishment like his own property. He can ruin me in a matter of days, if he wants. That's why I don't try and rub it in his face that I'm the real owner.

"I get to see my son at last." There's a hint of anger beneath the witty tone of Michael's voice. Even as an adult, I can't get rid of the immense feeling of fear at his outbursts.

One can never know the limits of his harm when he's mad. I'd rather be surrounded by a dozen first-degree murder offenders than have to deal with Michael in that situation. The first time Chloe's pictures with a boy appeared in a magazine—not while kissing or even holding hands, just walking together on a side walk—Michael got her fully naked and whipped her with his belt for half an hour straight in front of my mother, Zane, me, and the housekeepers. She had to be hospitalized for the deep scars on her skin at the tender age of fourteen. I have no doubt that incident triggered my mother's suicidal thoughts.

"I'm sorry, Father. I had a client to take care of." I hold my breath and glance at JJ pointedly, hoping he'll keep his mouth shut about Lindsay. He must have known from the pictures in tabloids that she's with Michael. Fortunately, JJ excuses himself without saying anything regarding the afternoon.

"Can I get you something to drink?" I ask Michael, opening the liquor cabinet.

"Whiskey."

I pour him generously from the twenty-five-year-old Chivas Regal and place the glass on the table in front of him. Without losing a second, I get myself a glass from the same drink and take a generous sip, so he can also start drinking without worrying about the possibility of having poison in his drink. If I'd done so many horrible things to people, like he has, I'd also suspect each and everyone around me of plotting my death.

"I'm having very important guests next weekend." He puts his glass back on the table and clasps his hands over my desk. "I want you to accompany me and do your best to entertain them."

"We can host a party here for their honor if you think it's appropriate. May I ask who they are and what kind of fun they'd prefer to have?" I take my place at the chair that's connected to the biofeedback machine and try not to glance at his face since he hates being stared at directly. For him, only people with power equal to him have the right to look him straight in the eye and there're only a handful of them in the entire world.

"The Russian Minister of Internal Affairs and his wife are coming for a special meeting. Get your best suites ready because they'll stay here for three nights. The media doesn't know it so you have to take extra precautions to keep their visit confidential. If anyone gets a whiff of their presence, I'll hold you responsible."

Oh, shit. I'll have to cancel all the appointments from the clients but still have to pay the loss payments to the employees. That'll cost me easily a hundred grand, not to mention the additional costs of catering and decorations. "Of course, Father."

"Make sure your best looking men and women are available during their stay and hire some additional prostitutes if you must. I want all of their wishes fulfilled to the smallest detail. I hope your Russian is up to par because you'll be their personal assistant throughout their stay."

"Yes, Father. I'll make sure they'll enjoy their time in Pleasure Extraordinaire."

"Lindsay will be here too, but make sure she doesn't get involved with anyone unless it's requested by the minister himself."

Lindsay? Fuck. With my bad luck, the minister will ask for only her for twenty-four hours long. I'll have to get in contact with her to warn her off accompanying Michael's guests. On the other hand, I have no idea how she can say no to Michael.

"I'll see to it." I work hard to listen to the details about the special guests, grab a pen and notebook to jot down their likes and dislikes, and ask questions to keep my thoughts away from Lindsay at least while in Michael's presence. The thought of Lindsay in the hands of some Russian jerk isn't something that can be ignored easily.

The Family

I run out of the PE building as if there're explosives in it, and in a sense, there are. Ace looked completely outraged, almost traumatized by the news of Michael's unannounced visit. I have no idea about their father-son relationship, but I have this nagging feeling that the two aren't exactly on their best terms.

That and my fear of facing Michael when I'm at my dirtiest, lowest, sluttiest makes me want to grow a pair of wings so I can fly away from PE's sex-filled walls as quickly as possible, although I know that he knows what I'm doing here.

I drive to my home to shower, change into normal clothes, which won't reveal majority of my body, and then text Taylor to ask about her plans for the evening.

Her reply arrives immediately. "I'm leaving for a dinner with Adriana. Adam has an errand to run and won't be coming until midnight. Help!"

My text: "Lindsay to the rescue! Make sure they serve margaritas wherever we're going. I'm planning to get her drunk and take her picture while she's making out with the bartender, then blackmail her to get her to behave nicely to you. It'll be fun!"

Taylor: "I can't say something similar hasn't crossed my mind. One problem, though. She's bringing her little son."

My text: "No problemo. We can cuddle with her son while she cuddles with the bartender. Btw, how is my nephew/niece doing in your tummy?"

"Hopefully growing," she replies, adding a smiley-face sign and the address of the restaurant. I want to assure her that this time she'll have a healthy baby and to offer her free babysitting for life, but what if she doesn't? If I'm feeling this insecure, how must she be feeling?

For some reason, I manage to arrive at the restaurant before Taylor and give Adriana an awkward hug. She and I probably exchanged only a few words during Taylor, and Adam's wedding reception and have never been alone.

"So, how are you?" I ask, trying to remember her son's name. Aiden, Jason?

"Not so well. The move has been going terribly. I have to deal with a lot of things with the new house and, as if I don't have enough on my plate, Felix refuses to sleep through the night."

Oh, Felix. Where did I get Aiden from? "He seems fine now. Huh, little boy? Aren't you the cutest baby in the world?" I coo and soften my voice while caressing his cheek with my finger, and he responds with the sweetest, heart-melting smile, revealing his four teeth, trying to grab my finger. Taylor arrives while Felix and I are exchanging intimate smiles, apologizes for her tardiness, and shakes hands with Adriana. As in no hugging. Huh? I have a suspicion whose fault it is.

"Would you mind taking care of Felix for a

second? I have to use the restroom," Adriana asks and Taylor and I both nod and wave our hands at her.

"Oh, please go and never come back, and leave your cute boy to us," I whisper to Taylor after I make sure Adriana is gone.

Taylor lifts the boy from his high chair and holds him in her arms, kissing his cheeks several times. "He's so sweet, I can kiss him all night long."

"I was thinking the same thing. So much the opposite of his mom. I'm sure she adopted him or exchanged babies in the hospital, because this cutie can't possibly have come out of her."

Taylor laughs and makes silly sounds to the baby, taping on his little nose with her finger, tickling him until his laughter fills the restaurant.

Adriana comes back, looking pale and shocked, and without any notice or permission grabs Felix out of Taylor's arms. "You should be gentle with him. He's not strong enough to be roughened up," she bellows. Roughened up? A few heads from nearby tables turn to our direction.

Taylor's face reddens in the instant. "I'm sorry. I didn't..."

"Come on, Adriana. What's your problem? She didn't do anything wrong," I say, angry at Taylor for apologizing for something she didn't do. She's giving Adriana reason to bully her.

"When's Adam coming?" Adriana asks Taylor, totally ignoring my comment.

"He's not coming," I answer her. "Must have better things to do than listening to your bullshit."

"Lindsay," Taylor yells at me, her eyes shooting fireballs of rage, and I wish she could yell at Adriana with the same anger. "Something came up at work in the last minute. He had to stay and deal with it," she explains to Adriana with a softer voice.

"Whatever, let's order," Adriana says, placing the boy back in his high chair, and grabs the menu. I seriously wonder what her problem with Taylor is. Some women have to deal with overly protective mother-in-laws; Taylor has to deal with a bitch as a sister-in-law.

In addition to food, I order a pitcher of margaritas, but neither Taylor nor Adriana want to share with me. Adriana claims to be still breastfeeding her son as an excuse, and Taylor uses the good old designated-driver excuse. So, I'm left with enjoying the drink all by myself.

I must say alcohol definitely helps me filter out most of Adriana's bullshit. I'm sure her husband must be an alcoholic in order to have enough libido to produce four kids with her. Taylor doesn't even dare smile at the baby's attempts to get attention. It's just sad. I hope she'll have her own baby and get a restraining order against Adriana so she pays for her rudeness with not being able to interact with her nephew/niece.

Through the end of the dinner, we three fall into silence. Adriana seems to have run out of her nonsense about her restaurant business and her children. Taylor wipes her lips with the napkin and leaves for the restroom, blowing an air-kiss to baby as she leaves. I don't miss Adriana's eye-rolling at Taylor's cute gesture. She seriously has issues with Taylor, and I'm going to find out the reason, even though I risk being excommunicated from all things related to Garnetts.

"Adriana, I'm very curious about something, and I hope you'll shed a light on my curiosity."

"Sure." She nods, looking intrigued about my question.

"What's your issue with Taylor, really?

Hmm? She has been nothing but nice to you the entire time. She loves your brother and has always been kind to your family. Why is it that you treat her like a piece of dirt?"

She freezes, can't even blink her eyes. Her boy cries loudly after nearly half an hour of sitting silently and cooing around as if he understood my attack on his mother. Even if Adriana decides to answer my question at this point, I won't be able to hear her words over the shrill screams of the boy.

Adriana murmurs something, and I can only make out "breastfeeding." I watch her throw a rather large shawl around her shoulders and chest and hold the baby in her arm, under the shawl. My ears haven't misheard her. She indeed said breastfeeding. Is breastfeeding in public allowed?

The boy's loud cry comes to a sudden halt, once he starts sucking on the nipple, at least that's what I think he's doing under the shawl. Adriana doesn't dare look at me and occupies herself with Felix.

When Taylor shows up again, her whole demeanor looks shifted. She looks sick, ghostly pale, and sad. Can she be offended by Adriana's breastfeeding in public? I can tell the people at the surrounded table are.

"What's wrong?" I ask when she doesn't speak and just watches Felix's hand moving up and down.

"I'm bleeding," she whispers almost inaudibly. I don't even see her lips moving.

"Oh, my god." Shit! Not again. When the witch of Adriana can't headcount her children, Taylor has to lose yet another one. I move my chair close to hers to hug her. Taylor collapses onto my shoulder and cries.

"What's going on?" Adriana asks, looking dumbfounded.

"She's having a miscarriage," I say, but immediately regret my openness. Taylor wanted to keep it secret from Adam, and now I'm revealing it to Adriana. Great job, Lindsay. I've probably given her yet another thing to use against Taylor.

"I'm sorry to hear that," Adriana says, and for the first time, there's sincerity in her voice. It's so unusual, it sounds as if someone else has spoken on her behalf.

"Would you mind if we leave now?" Taylor asks to Adriana, and Adriana simply nods. I pay the tabs and slip my arm around Taylor's waist as we walk to the parking lot. I realize I won't be able to drive, with the level of margaritas running through my veins. Taylor doesn't look like she can handle driving at the moment, either. So I call a cab, and together we drive to my condo.

I help her get into my bed, take off her shoes, and run to the kitchen to make us tea, while she cries silently. Putting two teabags of chamomile into the teapot, I carry it and two cups to the bedroom. Taylor is lying on her stomach, her head hidden under my pillow. I place the teapot and the cups on the nightstand and slip under the bedcovers beside her.

"This too shall pass," I find myself whispering to her. What a dumb saying, actually. Of course it'll pass, but who cares about the future right now? Why does it matter that the pain will diminish in the future? Maybe it won't? Maybe it'll just get worse if she keeps on having miscarriages. I caress her hair with my hand, incapable of doing anything else while watching her cry. She wants a child so badly, that's all she talks about and probably thinks about.

That must be the root of her problem. Of all our problems.

Wanting something so obsessively that everything else in her life stops mattering one way or another. If only she focuses her thoughts on something else and stops wanting a child so badly. She should stop counting the days of her menstruation cycle and, for the love of everything good in this world, stop buying those high-tech pregnancy tests that can detect pregnancy at a very early stage. Whoever claims that the technological advancements are for the good of humanity; here's the evidence to falsify your claim, served with disheartening tears of a hopeless woman.

After several minutes of crying, Taylor finally emerges from under the pillow and wipes her mascara-smeared face with her hand. "I'm starting to think I'm not supposed to be the mother a child. I'll most likely screw it up royally, that's why Mother Nature is trying to prevent it."

"As far as the reasons go, that's by far the stupidest. You'll make an excellent mother."

"How do you know that?"

"Because I've experienced your skills in person. You've been mothering me for all those years, in case you haven't noticed. As a child, even before I knew our aunt wasn't our mother, I loved you more than I loved her. You're everything a perfect mother can be. You're loving, caring, patient, and have I said loving? I love you as much as I could have loved our mother if I had the chance to get to know her."

"I'm glad I have you as my sister." She wraps her hand around my shoulder and pulls me in over her chest. "Did you know you saved my life before you were even born?"

"What?" I peek up at her and see a slither of smile curving up her lips.

"Yeah. When Mom was around five months pregnant with you, Dad wanted to have a vacation in Hawaii. It was my first time on a plane. I was giddy with excitement and didn't want to sit still in my seat. Just before the plane took off, Mom had a sudden cramp in her belly and starting screaming. The flight attendants couldn't do anything to ease her pain. At the end, Dad decided we had to leave. You'll not believe me but that plane, my dear, crashed into the ocean due to some mechanical failure, and no one survived. Later, when we went to hospital, the doctor said everything was fine with you. Mom always joked it was you kicking her as a warning to get out, but now I know you weren't actually kicking her, you were slapping her."

I start laughing and crying, as it's both funny and sad story. "Are you making it up? I've never heard of that before."

"I'm not making it up. You're the reason why I'm alive now. I may have lost our mother and my babies, but you and Adam are my rocks. I don't need anyone else as long as I have you and him."

Zane was right. Not everything is inherently bad. My existence helped save Taylor's life twice.

"That's the right attitude, but don't give up on miracles." I hug her, swallowing an enormous sob. "They really do come true."

We finally pay the necessary attention to the now-cold tea and drink it while watching Frat House. Apparently Taylor is the only female left on Earth who's not aware of the sexual pursuits of four hot college guys. Well until now, because tonight she's getting nothing but a heavy dose of Frat House until she remembers nothing about her miscarriage.

Around midnight, my cell beeps with message. I move over Taylor to get it from the nightstand and notice she's dozed off. Pulling the bedcovers over her, I palm my cell, switch off the TV and head to the kitchen.

The text is from Adam, asking about Taylor.

My reply: "Already sleeping after having

watched six episodes of Frat House. You'll have to hug your pillow to sleep tonight and maybe the rest of your life because she's now in love with the actors of the show."

His reply: "That marriage wrecker show must be banned at all costs! See you and hopefully my wife tomorrow for breakfast?"

The board members of Hawkins Media Group must be suffering from severe lack of attention from their wives. That's why they want to cancel the show. Now, that makes more sense than the lower ratings as an excuse.

I reply to him with a simple "Okay, good night." Just when I start to put the phone on the counter, I note an alert for another message. Not a new one but unopened. Curious and nervous, I tap on the screen and nearly drop the phone when I see the text is from Ace.

"I can't stop thinking about you."

Cold shivers run across my body as I read the words again and again. The afternoon with him was like a dream. Every minute in his arms felt like rebirth for my body. I bring my fingers over my lips, tasting myself, unsure if I imagined it all. The taste of his lips, his skin, his arousal. So unique and yet so familiar. Like everything else of him.

I realize the time he sent the message was ten fifteen, almost two hours ago. Why didn't I hear the cell beeping before? Has he been waiting for a reply from me? Maybe thinking I don't give a shit about him.

"What exactly can't you stop thinking about me?" I text back, hoping he hasn't given up on me.

"Your skin against mine, your lips on me, feeling you taking me inside you..." His message pushes me to groan. Almost. Oh my god. My inside muscles clench deliciously at his words. I want him desperately, hopelessly, madly, uncontrollably. If he was here with me right now, I wouldn't let him blink an eye throughout the night.

The Cruelty - ACE

I plop down on the couch of the room attached to my office and close my eyes. It's nine thirty in the evening, and I'm exhausted both physically and mentally. Lindsay and Michael hit heavily on my metabolism individually but after having been exposed to both of them the same day, I'm nothing but a sack of worn-out muscles.

The Russian envoy will be a problem I have to tackle before the party starts. Michael is ready to throw anyone directly into the wolf's mouth to get what he wants.

"Lindsay will be here, too, but make sure she doesn't get involved with anyone unless it's requested by the minister himself."

Unless it's requested by the minister? Jesus! The thought of being forced to watch Lindsay manhandled by some undeserving pig is enough to paralyze me. I have to make sure she won't be within a ten-mile radius of the minister for that matter. I'll inject her with the swine-flu virus if it's the only way to get her out of Michael and his guests' sights.

This is the first time Michael has asked me for help in entertaining his guests. Must be the confidentiality of the visit of the Russian minister. What is Michael after this time? I don't have the slightest idea of his business plans. I wouldn't know if he's thinking about starting up a TV channel over in Russia or getting into the East European drug world.

Zane would know, but I'd rather stay away from him. I still haven't forgiven him for going after Lindsay. Was she a one-time hook up for him? As much as I hate his guts for using women for only one-night-stands, I hope Lindsay is a long-forgotten name on the lengthy list of women he chases only for sex because I'm in no mood to deal with him right now. He'll likely end up setting Michael against me.

How about Lindsay? She wanted both Zane and me for the threesome. Is she attracted to him and maybe more? Fuck. The only woman I've met who has more to her than sexual qualities has to have something going on with Zane too. That's just wrong.

She hasn't pushed me away or called the police for my insult, although she had every right to. She saw my regret, my defeated and crushed soul and gave me a second chance. The way she opened up and gave herself to me loosened something in me, changed the rigidity in the depths of my soul.

I can feel her everywhere and smell her intoxicating scent as if she's right here, before me. My mind and my whole body are in a constant state of being at the brink of an orgasm, even though I had my release in her, marked her as mine without the barrier of a condom. The fire that comes with the close proximity of her body is still wild and destructive inside me, even though she's not here.

What is it with her that my mind can't push her out and my manhood can't stop throbbing for her, ignoring all the other available ladies?

What is she doing now? Hanging out with her friends? Enjoying some delicious food in a newly discovered restaurant? Drinking the night away? Watching TV? At least I know she's not with another guy, thanks to the contract she has with Michael. What an irony.

Is she thinking about me? Does she have the slightest idea of her effect on me? How, when they're pointed at me, her angry dark eyes can make everything else in my life worthless? How her touch can erase the damaging memories of my gloomy past? And when she's away, it's as if everything traumatic I've experienced doubles up and smashes me with a sledge hammer. Breaking me down. Does she know?

I pull my cell out of my pocket and text her, "I can't stop thinking about you." I stare at the phone for the next hours on high alert, blinking only when I must, nervous like a school boy sitting for a test for the first time, but nothing comes. No text, no call.

She's too much for my nerves to handle. Too intense, too tantalizing. This waiting, trying to second-guess her feelings for me make me physically tired. My muscles are worn-out and hurting as if I fought with the top MMA fighters.

Maybe I should just give up on her, ignore her existence, and forget that she ever existed. I already have enough problems on my plate, as it is. My men and my clients occupy enough of my life 24/7. Not to mention Michael and my siblings. Why bother adding another stress, another drop in the already full glass? Women shouldn't matter for me at this point of my life. I should go about them just like Zane. Hook up once or twice, then never look back. Much less hassle and more tranquility.

My phone beeps with a new text message from Lindsay and just like that my conviction vanishes.

"What exactly can't you stop thinking about me?"

I sit straight when I type my next message. "Your skin against mine, your lips on me, feeling you taking me inside you..." Only the truth, unadulterated, plain and straightforward, just like she appreciates it.

"I want to see you again."

I smile at myself, despite my anger at

Michael. "Breakfast tomorrow? At my place?"

"I'd like that."

I text her my address and slip the phone back into my pocket so I can doze off a few minutes before the night shift starts. Just when I close my eyes, my office phone rings and I jolt up on the chair. I run and grab the receiver. "Hello?"

"Ace, can you come over to my apartment now?" Chloe asks. Her voice sounds clogged, as if she's cried.

"Yeah, sure. What is it? Everything okay with you?"

"I'm leaving for Barbados tomorrow."

Oh, fuck! The last time she left for abroad unexpectedly was when Michael beat her up two years ago. She was forced to spend two weeks in Guatemala to hide the large bruises on her face and body from the paparazzi. My hand fists automatically. I inhale a long breath of anger. When is he going to stop abusing her?

I want to be there for her, yet I'm dreading seeing her ruined both physically and emotionally. "I'll be there in half an hour."

"Yeah, do that." She starts crying once the

words are out of her mouth. I'd have dogs fuck that man, if I could, for damaging my sister.

I assign Alexander to take over for the night shift while I'm away and drive directly to Chloe's apartment in Westwood. While she normally lives at Michael's mansion in North Hollywood, she managed to save money and bought herself a place she can call home and escape to whenever being around Michael becomes too much to handle.

The building has a doorman and front-desk-personnel, in addition to the video cameras all around for security, but no amount of protection will stop the damage Michael can give. I sign the visitors' sheet and take the elevator to Chloe's apartment.

Unlocking her door with my key, I rush through the foyer and find her in her bedroom. Only when I get to her side, I see the magnitude of the damage to her face. Her entire left cheek is purple, and the corner of her top lip is swollen with a lump the size of a golf ball, and there's dried blood all over her skin.

"What the fuck! What happened?" I reach out to hold her arm, but she yanks me away, crying in pain, and I see more bruises covering her arm.

"I don't know," she says between her sobs. "I was out with Dylan for dinner. We didn't do anything inappropriate, I swear. A few paparazzi took our pictures while we were leaving the restaurant. Next thing I know, Michael is waiting for me in my apartment." She burst into sobs and hides her face in her pillow. Why is he such a monster? And, why can't I do anything about it? Fuck me for watching him ruin my sister with each passing year.

"He did it in front of Dylan. He made him watch while he beat me up until I got knocked out. He threatened him not to move an inch or he'd ruin his family."

That fucking monster. "I'm sorry, Chloe." I dared touch her hair, caressing it slowly. "I promise you this will be the last time he'll ever touch you again."

"Don't give promises you can't keep." Her voice is coated with blame. More than Michael himself, she must be hurting because Zane and I have allowed him to do whatever he pleases with her. This has to come to an end. Even if it means the end of my business or my life as I know it, I'll make him stop ruining my sister.

She pushes my hand away, giving me an

angry glare, but all I can see is the hurt in her eyes. "How will you stop him? Zane couldn't do it. Mom died trying. How do you think you'll keep him away from me?"

"I'll find a way. This has to come to an end. He's getting worse every time."

She shakes her head, a painful smile twisting up her blood-coated lips. "Why now, Ace? This isn't the worst he's beaten me up. You didn't care the last time he messed me up so that I had to have hip surgery, remember?"

"I cared. Honest to god, I did, but I couldn't believe I had the power to stop him."

"You don't have it now, either. He'll ruin you. You'll wish you died."

"I don't care, Chloe. As long as you're safe, he can fuck me if he wants."

She throws herself at me, wraps her arms tightly around my neck, and buries her bruised face on my shoulder, crying her pain out. Can I do it? Can I really protect my sister from the devil himself? I should not only take her to a safe place so he can never find her again, but also find a way to stop him hurting others, too. Lindsay likely being the next one on his list.

Chloe packs a small bag with clothes, while I go out to find a public phone—a safer way as opposed to having my cellular being listened to by Michael's men—to call a close friend of mine from college to ask if she can have my sister over for some time until I figure out a way to keep her safe. Diana is at first puzzled to hear from me in the middle of the night, but readily accepts helping me out.

Without losing a minute, I drive Chloe to Diana's home in Camarillo, a small town on the way to Santa Barbara, away from Michael and all the paparazzi. Having heard my complaints about Michael enough times, Diana offers Chloe unlimited time to use her home. But I know better than to involve another innocent person for Michael to mess with, so, we agree on a two-week stay for now, until I come up with a permanent solution. Meanwhile, Michael will be thinking Chloe is in Barbados.

The Persuasion - ACE

Knowing Chloe is safe and out of Michael's reach at least for now, gives me peace of mind and helps me calm a bit. I throw myself on the bed. Tiredness is crushing down every bone of my body. The digital clock on the nightstand reads four thirty, reminding me that I haven't slept for nearly twenty three hours.

With Chloe occupying my thoughts, I arrange the pillow under my head and pull the covers over my body. She took after Mom in so many ways. Not only with her eyes and lips. The heartbreaking way she has given up hope and simply surrenders herself to Michael's abuses. As if she actually deserves every bit of torture he's doing to her. The dull look on her face. The lack of self-confidence and motivation to pursue her goals if she has any at all. Her total disinterest in life.

I'm afraid one day her end will be the same as Mom's. That'll be a tragedy I can't possibly survive. Mom's death didn't ruin me only because of Chloe's help. Unlike Zane, Chloe never treated me as an adopted brother. She loved me and showered me with the affection and love that I craved so much. She never withheld her encouraging smile, her motivating words, when it came to supporting my endeavors.

I, on the other hand, gave her nothing in return. I watched how Michael abused her without having the courage to do anything to stop him. More than a couple of times, she interfered while Michael was on me with full force, only to end up getting herself bruised and broken, but she did it. She tried to do something. Anything. Unlike Zane and me. She's stronger than both of us when it comes to protecting her brothers, but completely indifferent to her own wellbeing. As if she doesn't care what can happen to her. I wish I'll never have to see her broken and in tears again.

If I'm lucky, I'll find a way to get Lindsay away from Michael too. That, though, will be more challenging, because, before anything else, I'll have to convince her of his evilness.

My eyes fall closed with the images of Lindsay's face. As the minutes pass, though, her smooth skin turns dark with bruises and swells. My heart constricts with pain. I can't allow her to go through the same cruelty. I can't let Michael ruin another person.

My minds start drifting off slowly as darkness falls everywhere. The temperature drops. Shivers go through me as fear strikes my heart. I feel something bad is coming. Something terrible enough to make me want to die so I won't have to endure the same pain again. I hear muffled mumbles from far away. Then, all too suddenly, large hands capture my body, holding me still in place. "Calm down, now," the owner of the large hands whispers to my ear over and over again.

Air is pulled out of my lungs, and I work hard to be able inhale again. My hands reach for my throat to free whatever is covering my airway. I push. I struggle. I fight. Nothing works. I'm suffocating to the point of no return. I force my body against whoever is holding me with all my strength, and my eyes open abruptly. I inhale and exhale, shocked, staring around for the source of my distress. There's nothing, no one else in my bed. What the hell did I just dream about? I try to remember the details but all my mind can focus on is the sensation of asphyxiation.

The clock reads six thirty-five. My body is still trembling with the shock of it. I don't want to go back to sleep and have the same dream again. I get out of the bed, shower, and go out grocery shopping to fill my empty and neglected fridge. Very soon, the details of the stress while dreaming faints into nothingness, and I start going through the aisles in Whole Foods feeling excited that Lindsay will be with me in a couple of hours.

Having no idea what she likes to eat, I buy everything from cereal, eggs, pastries, bacon, to soup. I don't even know if she's a coffee, tea, or hot-chocolate person. So I add a sizable number of boxes of them too. In the end, the cart is filled to the brim, and I hurry to load everything in the back of my car.

Back in my loft, I get the coffee going while

pacing up and down in my living room. I haven't had a woman in my place for two years, since my last girlfriend. Though it feels strange having another woman inspect my private space, judging my style, furniture, or the lack of both since I like living minimalistic, I'm glad it's Lindsay, though, because at least she won't hide her true opinion behind some bullshit diplomatic remarks.

At nine o'clock sharp, my cell rings and I glance, smiling, at Lindsay's number flashing on the screen. I give her the code for the elevator and stride to the door to welcome her. My heart smashes against my chest as soon as the elevator doors open, and Lindsay emerges from behind. She's wearing her hair in a ponytail. Her body is covered beneath a dark-green leather jacket, in a red silk shirt, and tight blue jeans. It's official; her body has the same effect on me whether it's naked or covered.

"Very punctual. I like it." I tilt my head down once she's before me to kiss her, but she tactfully escapes from my lips and hugs me instead.

"I arrived ten minutes earlier but didn't want to come up too early." She passes through the doorway, sliding out of her jacket, and looks around.

I kick the door closed with one foot and grab her jacket out of her hold. "Why? You should have come."

"Why?" She shrugs, turning to me, a playful grin on her face. "I don't know. I guess I didn't want to witness another woman leaving your apartment."

I roll my eyes at her and hang her jacket in the closet. "Would you have been disappointed?"

"I won't answer that."

"You don't need to, because I know you would." I close the closet door, leap the distance between us in a flash, and slide my arms around her waist, lifting her up in my arms.

"Hey, hey, hey. What are you doing?" She smacks my arms and pushes my chest with some serious strength. "Put me down, right now!" I do as she orders, disappointed and excited at the same time. She might say no now, but she'll cave in soon. And that'll make it all the more satisfying.

"You promised." She lifts her forefinger up to my face with an unmistakable threat attached to her tone.

"I'm sorry. It's just hard to keep my hands to myself when you're around." I smile down at her, keeping my body in close proximity to her tiny physique. She trembles visibly but keeps her strict posture otherwise. "Hungry ... for breakfast?" I add, letting my smile broaden.

She shakes her head at my little word game, narrowing her eyes at me, and turns around to examine the living room.

"Have you recently moved?" she asks.

"No. I just don't like a lot of stuff. A couch, chairs, table, and a bed are all I need. I don't stay here often, maybe once or twice a month."

"Really? Why not?"

"My work is my life. PE has a lot of empty rooms anyway. It's easier to sleep there than commute from here to work every day." I guide her toward the kitchen and head to the coffee machine. "Can I get you something to drink?"

"Tea, if you have some."

I carry the shopping bag of the tea boxes for her to choose, and she picks up the one with apple cinnamon aroma.

"Smells good," I say and set the kettle on.

She opens the fridge without asking for my permission, goes through the unopened containers one by one, and takes out grapes and croissants. "Why do you keep these in the fridge?" she asks, showing the large pastry box. I shrug, having no idea of where else I should keep them. She warms up the pastry in the oven, and I decide to keep her in the dark about the fact that she's the first one to ever use it. In a matter of minutes, she gets herself comfortable enough in my kitchen that she orders me to sit down and sets about preparing a nice breakfast, worthy of a lazy Sunday morning.

Sliding over the chair beside me in front of the breakfast island, she sips from her tea, her eyes staring up at me. "You bought all that food for just for me, didn't you?"

"So what if I did."

"I don't mean it in a sarcastic way. I like it actually, except for the fact that you considered the possibility of me eating all that food."

I laugh, despite the presence of the food in my mouth. "I just wanted you to have options."

"Very accommodating of you."

I'd accommodate her in ways she could never even dream, if she'd let me. "Am I now?"

She nods, wiggling her eyebrows up and down. "Except in the bedroom."

"I'm sorry, what? I think I misheard you. You can't possibly be claiming I'm not accommodating in the bedroom because I distinctly remember providing you with a rare opportunity to be with two attractive men who know what to do in bed. Not to forget the series of orgasms you reached in one go. That is, in fact, the very definition of accommodating."

"You think you're attractive?" She seizes me up and down with one brow arched up, not revealing anything from her assessment. Come on. I know she likes what she sees, yet she has to play with me like a toy.

"Is that what you got from what I said?"

"That and something about a series of orgasms." She glances up directly into my eyes for the briefest of a second, blushing, and drops her gaze to her plate. She's embarrassed and that's so adorable, I consider spreading her up on the breakfast island to deepen her blushing.

"Now you're stuck with the memories." I shake my head playfully. If anyone is stuck with those memories, that'd be me. Even the trauma of my sister isn't strong enough to shake away the tornado of the afternoon I had with Lindsay, in Lindsay, and on Lindsay. I lick my lips, wishing I had the taste of her orgasm on my tongue again. That'd sweeten my bitter coffee.

Her hand slides down to her thigh, and I notice she's squeezing her legs together. How unjust is it that women can be subtle about their arousal, but we men have to deal with some big and obvious evidence? Just like the one I'm sporting right now. If I don't do anything about it soon, she'll spot it any second. Not that I'm ashamed of her sexual power over me or anything. But, if she finds out and decides not to do anything about it, that'll be a big blow to my ego.

I pull my shirt down casually while sipping from my coffee, which tastes too bitter, but I drink it anyway. Lindsay has been nibbling on the same edge of the croissant for more than ten minutes now. Either she's a picky eater or just nervous. I'll go with the second excuse for the reason for her lack of hunger.

I remember Michael's words about the Russian envoy and Lindsay. I should warn her to stay away from the party, but on the other hand, I don't want to ruin this calm silence I'm sharing with her. She crosses and uncrosses her legs, and at one point brushes the side of her thigh against mine. I hear her inhaling sharply, although she tries to hide it by sipping more tea.

"How are we going to do this?" I ask. I can't date her, but I can fuck her, although I don't know exactly under which circumstances or how often. Michael didn't mention anything about the limits of the payment he took over for Lindsay's visits to PE. Not that I'll charge her anything for the fun I'll have with her, but I'm sure she won't want to cross the lines of that fucking contract. She's so goddamn adamant about staying true to some arbitrary rules Michael can, and without doubt will, violate.

"I won't sleep with you today if that's what you're asking. It seems that I can only use PE services once a week."

"What if, as the owner of PE, I offer you unlimited complimentary service, at your will?"

She sighs and rests her head on her hand, playing with the teaspoon. "That's exactly what Michael is against. He doesn't want me to date or have anything else with a guy. I'm already going against that rule as is. According to him, I must sleep with a different guy every time I'm at PE."

"Did he seriously demand that from you?"

"Not directly, but through his assistant."

"What's his reasoning? His main point for hiring you as his girlfriend is to cover up his homosexuality. I'm obligated by law to keep the information about my clients off the record, anyway. What's his deal if you want to fuck the same guy over and over as long as it remains a secret?"

She has no answer to that. Shrugging, she finally gives up on the croissant, leaves the empty cup on the counter, and slides down from the chair. Did I upset her? Is she leaving already?

"Please, don't go. I won't insist anymore. It's your decision." I reach up and hold her shoulder tentatively. She doesn't push me away or attempt to leave, just stays beside me without moving, her eyes glued to mine. She's trying to decide, I can see it in the deep frowning of her brows. If she stays, she'll risk betraying Michael's trust. But if she goes, she'll lose a possibly one-time chance to connect with me. Only, she doesn't know I have no intention to leave this as one time and am ready to give her a dozen more chances to connect or do anything else she wants to do with me.

"Let me show you the terrace." My loft might be missing furniture, but it makes up for it with a large terrace and a breathtaking view of L.A. She nods, and I take her hand, guiding her to the open air.

She gazes at the terrace with a wide-open mouth. "Oh, my god. My entire apartment is smaller than this."

I pull a chair for her and sit on another next to hers. "This is my favorite part of the loft."

"How did you find this place? You must be paying a lot for the rent."

"No, I inherited it from my mother and moved in when I turned eighteen. Michael didn't want to support me financially anymore, so I rented out the rooms to college students to make a living. At one point, we were ten, using all three bedrooms and the living room, but I didn't care. It was cheap for the renters, and I earned my money. That's all that mattered."

"What did you major in?"

"I enrolled in the medicine department at USC but failed miserably. I don't know why I'd thought I could be a doctor in the first place. Even after I switched departments to business, I couldn't make it. Reading isn't really my thing."

"Why? Have you been diagnosed with some form of reading disabilities?"

"No, I haven't. I always got the best grades back in the school. Then again the teachers were easy on me because of Michael. So, maybe I indeed have a physical problem, but it doesn't matter anymore."

"How can you say that? Reading is the most important skill you can learn."

I shrug and rest my back against the chair, spreading my knees wide apart. "It physically hurts my brain when I have to read."

"Oh. Sorry, I didn't mean to offend you."

"I don't easily get offended. And, you can't offend me even if you try." I reach up to caress her cheek, drop my hand on hers, and lace my fingers through hers.

She looks down at our entwined hands with a faint smile on her face. "You can't read well but you're clever enough to build a million-dollar business. That's admirable. How did you do it?"

"Like every other business. By starting small."

Staring up at me, she knits her eyebrows together. "Explain."

I laugh. She's the definition of inquisitive.

"You know. We went to clubs and hunted down horny, rich cougars, and asked for money in return for our favors."

Her jaw drops, her eyes growing large with shock, and she yanks her hand away from mine. "You worked as a prostitute and picked up clients at clubs?"

"What's the difference between what I do now and what I did back then? Both involve sex in exchange for money. Why does it matter that now I get to do it in a fancy building that I own?"

"I guess nothing," she says, defeated. But, I know what really worries her.

"Don't worry. I didn't do it. The two times I tried it, I mean having sex with a lady in exchange for money, I couldn't get hard."

She shakes her head, smiling, perhaps not believing the truthfulness of my confession. "Really?"

"Yeah, really. When I looked at their eyes, I saw loneliness and sadness. They reminded me too much of Irene, my adopted mother. She always had the same expression in her eyes. I simply couldn't do it."

"I heard she died of cancer," she says.

"That's a lie Michael spread to gain more sympathy from the public. Irene didn't have cancer. She committed suicide."

"Oh." She remains quiet, except for her audible breathing, although her face looks like dozens of questions are trapped behind her lips. It's a sore topic. The last years of Mom's life and how she left Chloe, Zane, and I alone in the hands of a monster.

"You need to decorate here with flowers here," she says. I smile, relieved by the change of the conversation.

"Maybe someday ... if I can find a worthy lady to take care of them."

She snorts, holding my gaze, and lifts her hand to rest it on my thigh. I try very hard not to flinch from her touch so close to my privates. My pulse quickens in an instant. "You don't need to wait that long. Just hire a housekeeper."

She leaves her hand there, drawing the infinity symbol over and over with her index finger on my jeans. The warmth of her palm sends pleasant jolts across my body. She's with me, alone in my apartment. No one can stop us from spending the day fucking each other. No one except her.

Having her so close to me is a burden to my senses. She smells of roses, not the scentless ones sold in supermarkets but the real ones that grow in the garden. I fill my lungs with her fresh and fragrant scent. Her skin is glowing under the sunlight. She's so easy on the eyes, sweet, yet sensual. The desire to kiss every corner and contour of her body hits me suddenly. The image of having her naked on my bed, waiting and begging for me to please her, makes my cock stiffen and pulsate beneath my jeans. And the fact that her small, warm hand is so close to it...

Why is she so goddamn unbending about doing the right thing? Why can't she just unzip my pants and take my throbbing member into her hands, into her mouth? My chest tightens at the realization that I can't have her today and only god knows when I can feel her naked skin against mine.

I'm too tense from having to keep my hands off of her, and with every passing minute, my erection is bordering on painful. If I don't do something about it, I'll lose control and take her under me here, out in the open, and she won't have a chance to say no.

I gently grab her hand and lift it, very cautious not to let her presence get into me more than it already has.

"I'll be back," I say and stand. In the last second, though, I lean down to steal a brief kiss from her lips. She doesn't stop me, but doesn't kiss me back either. She's hesitant and maybe a little scared. I don't know, but pushing her won't do it for me.

With the taste of her lips in my mouth, I hasten to the bathroom and close the door behind me. I quickly unbutton and unzip my jeans. My erection springs out of my boxers with pre-cum already leaking. I palm it, feeling it getting bigger in my hand and start rubbing it up and down roughly, imagining it's Lindsay's hand squeezing it.

She'd lick her lips seductively, hinting at her dirty plans for me. Maybe she'd move down, slowly kissing her way on my chest down to my hips, settling on her knees in front of me. She'd tease me endlessly, kissing my shaft and balls for a long time before finally taking me into her mouth. I'd have to fight the urge to come all too quickly.

I stroke myself harder and faster as my mind trails off to the memories of the previous afternoon

I had with her; how her body arched and tensed with the pleasure I gave her, and her inside muscles pulsated as I pumped deep into her. How she surrendered to me completely and gave me a piece of herself.

I've known her for only a few weeks now, yet in that little time she managed to occupy my thoughts and infiltrate them so much so that I can't pay attention to anything else. If I didn't know any better I'd think she held me spellbound with some dark and dangerous love potion.

Collapsing on the wall behind me, I clamp my eyes shut, picturing Lindsay lying naked on my bed, her legs pulled up together at her knees. I'd spread them wide apart and watch her squirm as I enter her.

I hear the door unlatch and snap my eyes open. Lindsay is standing, shocked, at the doorway.

"Busted. I knew you were hiding here to do it," she says, holding the doorknob, staring at my hand rubbing myself.

I turn, leaning on my shoulder, to give her a better view of what I'm doing, what she's actually here to see. "Yet you didn't shy away from showing up."

She can't give me a reasonable explanation for why she decided to catch me red-handed, besides the obvious one. I push my hips forward, stroking myself with a leisurely speed now, for her to enjoy the show.

She has one foot in the bathroom and the other one on the other side of the doorway as if ready to flee, but she doesn't move. She's paralyzed, looking uncertain of what to do, maybe trying to convince herself to get the fuck out of my apartment. Her logic must be screaming at her to run, reminding her of the contract she signed with Michael. But something keeps her here and keeps her eyes glued to the slow movements of my hand. I feel triumphant at every additional second she chooses to stay with me, and that I have that effect on her.

"Come here," I say. She doesn't follow my wish and instead smirks at me. Expecting otherwise would be just foolish. Her body, however, tells a different story. Her chest is moving up and down with short breaths. She rolls her lips together and then bites the lower one.

I push my jeans down, sliding out of them, and walk toward her with slow steady moves, my hand still rubbing myself. She keeps standing unmoved, except for her eyes that are skimming me up and down in panic.

"Unbutton your shirt," I ask with a softer tone. She looks up at my face, almost begging with her eyes to not take it any farther. She must have realized her foolish mistake by now, but can't find it in herself to put a stop to it. That's why she's throwing me the ball; to end it. Only, I have no will whatsoever to do anything but take it to the next level. "I said unbutton your shirt. If you don't do it nicely, I'll rip it apart."

"Oh, god," she whispers almost inaudibly but breathes loudly between her parted lips. I halt two feet from her to stifle the urge to push myself down on her face and capture her mouth.

"Now," I say softly again, but she startles as if I yelled at her.

"I... I shouldn't... We shouldn't," she mumbles.

I smile, taking courage from having her still with me, despite her pretended unwillingness. She's fighting an internal struggle, and I'll make it easy for her. I take the last step and stand right in front of her. Our bodies are within brushing distance. Slowly, I lift my hand, find the last button of her shirt above her navel, and unbutton it. Her eyes close. Her chest stops moving.

My fingers crawl up and reach for the next button. I lean down, inhaling her scent, letting it intoxicate my already stoned mind, and whisper in her ear, "Nobody will know it. I'm the same man you made love to yesterday. Nothing changed. I'm no more inclined to reveal your secret with Michael now than yesterday."

She sighs. I caress her soft skin with my thumbs just before I undo the third button right below her bra. Her nipples tighten beneath her shirt. I notice her hands form fists at either side of her body.

"You know Michael's demands are baseless," I continue. "You only promised him that you won't do anything that will risk others knowing about his secret. Nothing more. This won't put him at risk. I haven't talked about his homosexuality to anyone for the last twenty five years. I won't start spreading it now."

"Please," she murmurs.

Please, what? Please, take me now? Please, let me go?

She opens her eyes and stares up at me with a tender look that I see for the first time on her face. No more frowning brows, fiery eyes or tightly pursed lips that are guarding her true self, but only a childlike, mellow, and vulnerable expression softening her beautiful features. I'm taken aback for a moment. My mind is running wild trying to absorb the unmasked emotions glowing on her face. A truly untouched beauty mixed with fragility and guilt. Why?

A powerful feeling of protection rushes over me and clenches my gut agonizingly, when the possibility of Lindsay being crushed and abused at Michael's hands floods my mind.

"It's not wrong." I unbutton the last button, pull down the red bra covering her breasts, and run my hands on her erect nipples. "You come to my home, knowing you'll be alone with me, and then walk into my bathroom, knowing what I'm doing in here. You're wearing this goddamn sexy lingerie. You can't tell me you don't want me."

She averts her eyes in shame. I squeeze her breasts and push her against the wall, leaning down toward her face. My lips trace a path on her face, brushing every inch of her forehead, down to her cheeks, and stop at her mouth. "I want you,

Lindsay. I haven't wanted any woman in my life like I want you. I don't care if it's against some arbitrary contract or the federal constitution. I just want you. Please, let me love you. Give me a chance to show you how much I crave you."

At last, she gives in and wraps her arms around me. Her lips crash into mine with urgency, and she kisses me possessively. I push her shirt off her shoulders, then her bra. She angles her body to mine, pressing her breasts against me. I quickly take off my t-shirt, tossing it aside, and feel her soft skin against mine. She squirms when our lips find each other again and our tongues fight for dominance.

Her jeans and panties are the next, and soon she's fully naked before me, just like me. I don't have any patience left in me. I must have her now. I consider the various ways I can take her. In my bedroom, in the living room, on the couch, or on the floor. Her back against the wall and her legs around my hips will give me the pleasure of seeing her face while I fuck her. She can watch herself being fucked if I take her from behind against the sink in front of the vanity mirror. But my cock only demands to be inside her, the deeper the better.

I release her lips and pull my head up enough

to keep myself from kissing her back again. "Bend down and hold your ankles."

Without needing to ask me anything for a clarification or an explanation, she flips around, spreads her legs, and crouches down, forming a perfect upside-down V shape with her legs in front of me. My cock goes impossibly stiff with desire at the sight of her spread cheeks and wet pussy all exposed. She pushes her ass up against me and tilts her head to the side to glance up at my face. She's impatient, and I reward her for her hunger with slowly easing into her. She's so wet and ready for it; her sex pulls me in without any effort from me to thrust.

We both groan when I hit balls-deep into her. I hold her hips to keep her in place as I slide in and out of her. Her gasps and moans echo in the four walls of the bathroom. The louder she gets, the harder I thrust. At one point, she loses her balance and her hands land on the floor, her ass still up against my groin. I slip my hands around her belly and lift her hips until her feet aren't touching the ground, while I continue driving into her with steady strokes.

She inhales loud, shaky breaths. Her body is light and soft, a toy for me to play with. Her legs move up and wrap around my waist. Fuck it if this isn't the strangest position I've ever had sex in. I'm standing straight, she upside down, facing the floor, her legs tight around my waist, and we're connected in the most arousing way. There's a constant moan coming from her throat accompanied by my name every now and then. I thrust her harder each time "Ace" rolls out of her lovely mouth.

Too soon, I find myself fighting against an imminent release, and I'm not even sure if she's coming or anything close to it.

She circles her hips, rubbing her clit against my balls. I slow down to let her do whatever she needs to find her own release.

"Don't you fucking stop," she yells and glances up at me with threatening eyes. Her legs squeeze around my waist to add to her warning. I have no other way but to comply with her wish.

Thrust, moan, breathe, thrust, moan, breathe.

Our skins are slick with sweat, all my senses on high alert. Lust blurs my mind, pushing me close to insanity. She's everywhere and everything I feel. I close my eyes; she's still there. The smell of our fucking fills up my nose, leaving no room for anything else. I can't feel where my body ends and hers begins. She's me and I'm her.

Before I can even think straight, I lose it. Everything I thought I was slips away into nothingness in the instant I hammer my release into her. I freeze and realize she's not moving either. Only when I open my eyes, I notice I've shut out all the noise, including Lindsay's sobs.

"Fuck you. Fuck this," she swears one after another and loosens her legs around me. I ease out of her and help her get her feet on the ground. Rather than standing, she collapses on the floor, still crying and mumbling curses. She'll catch a cold on the chilliness of the cold floor, but that doesn't seem to bother her.

"What's it, baby?"

"I'm not your baby." She rolls on her back and throws her arms over her face, panting and crying.

When I scoot down, she flinches up to her feet and flees from me. I get seriously worried as I watch the door bang loudly behind her. Did I come too fast? Did she tell me to stop and I didn't hear her? Did I hurt her? Is that why she's mad?

I jump up and follow her into my bedroom. She moves over the bed, slips under the bedcovers, and continues crying silently. It must be the contract. She must be feeling guilty for breaching a non-existent rule by having sex with me. If only I could make her see Michael is the last person on earth worthy of her loyalty.

"I'm sorry I pushed you into something you didn't want." I kneel on the bed, plop behind her body, and pull the covers away from her head. "You have no fault in this. It was entirely my doing. If Michael ever finds it out…"

"I'm not crying about that." She sobs and pushes the cover back over her head.

My hand moves over to her shoulder, though I don't know if I'm allowed to touch her. "Why, then? Tell me. I need to know."

"You were right," she says between loud sobs. "I shouldn't have had sex with you for the second time."

Her reply leaves me more puzzled than anything else. When did I ever tell her not to have sex with me twice? "I don't understand."

"You told me the day we first met. I shouldn't have sex with the same man more than once unless I have total control over my emotions. I can clearly see now, I have no control whatsoever over my emotions, thoughts, or my body."

A smile forces its way on my lips despite my worry over Lindsay. "You're not alone in this. I'm the same. I've been a total mess since the day I met you. The sex only made it worse."

She raises her head above the covers, turns her head, and gives me a questioning glance. "Are you toying with me?"

"Of course not." I crawl under the covers to feel her naked skin against mine, slide my arm beneath her arm, cupping one breast, and lower my head to kiss her shoulder. Her sobs turn into gasps and squirms, and she trembles in my arms and pushes her ass against my flaccid member.

"You amaze me, Lindsay Doheny, and you scare me. You drive me insane with your unpredictability. You encourage me to be a better man. You're the first woman who has ever made me feel jealous of other men. You're the most straightforward person I've ever known. You're giving, kind, generous, funny, smart, protective, sexy, beautiful, vulnerable, yet very strong. For the first time in my life, I'm thankful to Michael. For bringing you into my life. You're my dream woman come true."

"Wait, wait, wait. You're insulting me while buttering me up. For one, I'm not unpredictable and definitely not scary. Who do you think I am? Chucky's Bride?"

"Have you seen yourself in the video with Macey Williams? I think Chucky's Bride would look like an angel next to you." I laugh and squeeze my arm around her tighter, because she's slapping my hand and trying to escape from my hold. "I'm kidding. I'm kidding."

She pinches my arm so hard, I have to flinch my hand away. Taking advantage of my pain, she jumps up on me, straddling me with her legs. Her knees press painfully against my ribcage, and I let out a scream. "How about this? Ace Hawkins, you're an absolute ass, an arrogant dick, a voyeur, promiscuous, opportunist, obnoxious, and manipulative."

I lift my hand to her face, brush her cheek, and then draw her down against my body so I can kiss her. She surrenders, softens the hold of her knees, and kisses me back. Then, easing back to look at me, she adds, "And I can't stop having dreams about a future with you. I'm a lost case, I know." Her eyes search my face for a reaction, perhaps a serious one that reciprocates her honest feelings for me, but I can't help laughing. "Just like I said, you're an absolute ass." She smacks my chest and starts to move down.

I wrap my arms around her to hold her in place. "I'm sorry. I'm just caught by surprise. I'm glad you dream about me, because I dream about you all the time."

"What dreams?"

"You know, dreams."

"Sex dreams?"

"Yeah."

She rolls her eyes and smirks. "It's not the same. Oh, men. When will your small heads stop ruling over your big heads?"

She rolls down over to the bed and I let her go. She curls up against me, resting her face on the pillow beside me, gazing at me with curiosity. I can stay naked in bed with her just like this for the rest of my life, her soft curves pressing against my skin, and I won't complain. With her, I can shut out all the problems, my past horrors, disappointments, losses. They stop running amok in my mind when Lindsay is with me.

She touches my shoulder gently, then waves her hand at my face. "Hey, are you still there? Don't tell me you're having a sex dream right now."

"I kind of am. I was thinking how completely happy I'd be if I got to spend the rest of my life naked in bed with you."

A breathtaking smile broadens her lips, and she lowers her eyes, her smooth skin flushing a deep red instantly. I guess this was more of the response she was fishing for.

"God, I want you." I catch her neck and pull her in to kiss her senseless. Our tongues fight to claim each other's mouths. Her teeth bite me playfully; her lips suck with passion. As our kiss deepens, she lifts her leg and hooks it up around my hip. Her hand grabs my semi-hard cock and rubs it along the lips of her moist pussy. As soon as it gets to its full length, she guides it inside her body. Her irises roll to the back of their sockets, and she arches her head back, gasping as I fill her up. Her pussy is creamy wet, soft, and cushiony, and wraps around my cock tightly like a hand.

She's so fucking hot; although I came not longer than fifteen minutes ago, I'm ready to burst into her now. I slide my hand down and press my thumb against her clit. She groans and turns her head down to watch our fucking. Her eyes are heavy. Her lower lip is trapped between her teeth. Lust is giving her face a new dimension and intensifies her beauty.

Sex has always been mechanical for me. Only about getting my dick into a pussy and some hard friction until I'm done. Never have I felt astonished or even slightly interested by the sight of my lovers. None of them caused my heart to pump like it'll jump out of my chest. Lindsay, however, awakens all my senses, alerts my mind and pushes my heart to its limit. What is it with her?

I thrust into her hard and draw circles around her clit with my thumb because there's no way I can hold it for longer.

"Oh, god. I'm coming." Her mouth remains open as her body stills. The exquisite view of her losing herself pushes me toward my own release, and I drive my thick load into her pulsating sex. My heart beats loudly in my ears. My body is fuming with heat as my lungs demand more air.

The physical strain of having sex twice with only a few minutes break after two hours of sleep hits me full force, and I roll on my back, moaning like a shot animal. The pillow draws me inside it with an unimaginable power, and my eyes fall closed. Darkness covers everything, including Lindsay's musical voice.

When I wake, I feel lost, disoriented. Have I dreamed everything? Murmurs of a female come from the living room, and my memory is instantly filled with the flashbacks of Lindsay. I can't have possibly dreamed it all, because the fresh images running wild in my head can't be the product of my dull mind.

My head still feels heavy. I don't know how long I slept but I can definitely use a few more hours. I head to the bathroom and get a quick, cold shower to wake the rest of my body up. I may need to go to work, but I won't as long as Lindsay wants to spend the rest of the day with me, even if the entire PE building catches a fire.

After drying myself, I comb my hair and wrap a towel around my hips. Lindsay is wearing my t-shirt and sprawled on the couch, talking on the phone. The sight of her bare legs sends all my blood pooling in my groin again. Her eyes drop to the towel—the part covering my crotch to be exact—once she notices me.

"Can't it wait until tomorrow?" she asks to

whomever she's talking on the phone. "I see. Okay." She sighs as she disconnects and places the phone on the coffee table. "Hey, sleepyhead. I thought you passed out." She sits up, letting her eyes wander over my chest, and I smile at the appreciation visible in her expression. I settle on the couch beside her and put my arm around her shoulder. She welcomes me with a soft kiss and slides both her arms around me as tightly as if I might escape, reflecting my own urge to have her close.

I ease back a little to admire her face, glowing pink cheeks, smiling lips, and twinkling eyes. No sign of anger or disappointment on her face. Good. "You're beautiful."

"So are you." She runs her fingers through my wet hair, playing with its curls.

"Who were you talking to?"

Her body stiffens. The smile freezes on her face. Her whole demeanor changes with my questions. "Edric. Michael wants to see me today."

My body reacts exactly the same way to her response. What does he want from her? I have a nagging suspicion that it's about the Russian envoy. I have to make sure Lindsay doesn't get involved with them. "Lindsay, I have to tell you something, and I need you to believe every word I say. I care a lot about you, and I don't want you getting hurt."

The mask she usually wears falls back onto the contours of her face. Her brows knit together, forming deep lines in between. Her lips are a tight line.

"Michael told me about some very important guests he'll have next weekend. The Russian Interior Minister and his wife. He wants me to entertain them over at PE. My understanding is that they won't be content with just exotic food and fine music. They'll also want sexual pleasures, which I'm more than happy to provide them with my staff. However, Michael implied something that I think you have a right to know."

Her chest stops moving. She stares at me wild-eyed. I think she knows what I'm about to say. "If the Minister wants you as a sexual partner, Michael won't decline his request."

"Oh, god." She pulls her hands away from me and cups her now red cheeks.

"You can get away from it. Say you're sick. Get really sick if you must but don't join that party.

He's not the person you think he is. He physically abused Chloe, Zane, and me for years long and still does. Irene killed herself because she couldn't take it anymore. He treats his employees with disrespect and hostility. You have to protect yourself from his abuses. Better stay at your home with a high fever or a broken leg than be around Michael's clients, because Michael has no limits when it comes to satisfying the clients he works with to get what he wants."

"What if I can't convince him, what if he forces me, are you going to be at the party?"

"Yes, I will. I must be present as the owner of PE and his son. But, please, I'm begging you, find a very good excuse and save yourself from the pain."

She nods several times. Panic tenses her muscles all over, and her body shakes visibly. "I have to go now. Michael is expecting me."

"Okay, I'll get ready quickly and drive you."

"No. Someone might see me in your car. It's better nobody knows about us. I'll call a cab."

"Good call."

She hurries to the bathroom and comes back fully clothed. I hold her jacket as she slides in and hug her tightly before opening the front door for her. "Call me afterwards."

"I will," she says and strides into the elevator.

The Truth

What have I gotten myself into? I must have the perception of a five-year-old for not having seen what kind of manipulative and abusive person Michael is. But, a part of me whispers, what if Ace is the manipulative one? Ace is sweet and handsome, and sexy as hell, and I might know him physically better than anyone else, but the fact remains that I don't know his personality any more than I know Michael's. Ace might have a secret agenda or some unresolved issue with Michael and might be trying to get back at him through me—just like Zane tried—although I don't know what exactly he'll gain by preventing me from entertaining Michael's guests.

Maybe he's upset that he didn't receive the same affection and treatment from Michael as Zane and Chloe got as his biological children. He might be upset about some financial disadvantages he had or is having while Zane and Chloe live well off.

Ahhh. Why can't I just see into people's minds?

After I get into the cab and give the driver the address of Hawkins Media Group headquarters, I pull out a pen and paper to make a list of signs I observed about Michael to decide if he might or might not be the narcissist, obsessed with power and control, Ace and Zane claim him to be.

- Michael has never ever treated me with disrespect. He has met all the requirements of the contract from his side, and not just that, changed a term to accommodate my need for physical closeness with men.

- Edric admires him and the other

employees I met never mentioned or even hinted at any kind of hostility at work.

Just these two observations prove that Ace lied to me about one thing; Michael's disrespect toward his employees. Why wouldn't he have lied about anything else? If I'm honest with myself, I'm still undecided about his involvement in the coconut oil incident during my sexual encounter with Zane.

- Irene Hawkins' death. It says she died of cancer on Michael's Wikipedia page. Can the medical records of someone's death be corrupted so easily? I remember seeing a picture of her looking very sick and with a scarf covering her head, like patients undergoing chemotherapy do to hide their baldness. That again falsifies Ace's claim.

- Michael's persistence to hire me and pay me for being his girlfriend. The money I'm receiving, the car I own, the dresses, and jewelry. The job that I have. Why did he choose to over-compensate me when I openly and clearly told him I'd date him without getting anything in return? I understand his need as a businessman to make me sign a contract, but the things I receive in return can't be a simple gesture of generosity. Almost two frigging million dollars. I still fail to see why he specifically picked me to begin with, but it's evident that he's giving me more than he gave his previous pretend girlfriends. Much more.

This point supports Ace's claims, though vaguely.

Before I can add another point to my list, the cab stops and I look out to see Hawkins Media Group written in golden letters. I pay the driver, put the paper and pencil back into my bag, and climb out of the cab. Although my brief analysis about Michael proves his innocence, it didn't help with my anxiety. My hands are sweating, my legs shaking.

Why does Michael want to talk to me now? Why can't he wait for tomorrow? He might be leaving for a business trip, I tell to myself to calm down as I climb the stairs. My body feels as if it's drained of all blood as I suddenly look up and notice the street number of the building.

5727.

I want to kick myself in the ass for not having noticed the sevens in it before. Not just one but two. Does it mean double the trouble or just that they negate each other? But five plus two is also seven. Oh, god. If I was worried a second ago I'm terrified now, having proof of the dreadful minutes ahead of me.

I bite my lip, trying to remember Zane's words about my illogical belief in seven's bad luck. He wasn't all wrong when he said the things related to seven I thought were bad were actually good in the end.

This isn't the fifteenth century or some dictatorship where wealthy and powerful people do as they like. We live in a democracy. Each individual has rights. Michael can't force me into anything. I can call the police and sue him on the spot. He can't hurt me.

With renewed confidence, I walk through the door and step into the elevator. Julie nods with a smile as I enter her office. "Hello, Lindsay. How are you?"

"I'm good. I've come to see Michael."

"I'll let him know." She dials the phone without looking at the number pad. "Mr. Hawkins, Lindsay is here." My heart leaps at the mentioning of Michael's name.

Calm down, Lindsay, before you make a fool of yourself!

As soon as Julie nods, I move toward Michael's office and knock on the door briefly.

"Come in." His voice comes as a muffled sound.

You can do it. Just get a grip on yourself. "Hi, Michael. Edric told me you wanted to see me." My voice trembles as I say the last two words. Shit.

He smiles his usual heart-warming, genuine smile, and I find my body relaxing a bit.

"Come in. Sit down. I have some news."

"Okay." I take my seat at the chair in front of his majestic desk and clasp my hands together. Good thing he didn't try to shake hands, or his hand would be soaked with my sweat.

"I have another meeting in fifteen minutes. That's why I have to make this quick. I'll have an important guest next weekend, and I want you to accompany me for the full weekend during their visit. See, he's bringing along his wife, and I think she'll enjoy having a lady friend your age, rather than me."

I force myself with all my strength to keep myself from giving away the hurricane going on inside me. All my senses are telling me to follow Ace's advice. I won't be going against the contract.

I won't cause him bankruptcy by not attending one event with him. The only decision I need to take is whether I should decline now or later. Letting him know about my unwillingness now is better for him because he'll have more time to find a replacement.

I take a long breath and tell him the first words that come to my mind, "I'm very sorry but I can't. Why don't you invite Chloe instead? She'll surely be more fun than I would. She knows more stuff about exquisite locations and stores in L.A. than I'll ever know."

To my astonishment and relief, the friendliness of his demeanor doesn't disappear. "Why exactly can't you help me out?"

The problem with never telling a lie at all is coming up with a sound excuse on the spot, like I'm experiencing at this moment. "Family problems."

"May I ask what family problems you're having? I may offer a solution."

I swallow. Lies attract more lies, don't they? There's no end to it once you start. That's another reason why I prefer staying clear of lying. Until now, that is. "I can't talk about it, but Taylor is having health issues, and I don't feel comfortable leaving her alone when she needs me most."

He plops his elbows on the desk and laces his fingers together, resting his chin on his face. "Funny thing. You deemed it appropriate to leave her alone for the entire morning and afternoon today, but you can't spare two days for me a week from now."

How does he know that? Is he following me? Zane's words the day I met him for the first time echo in my mind. "He'll follow your every step. You'll not have the freedom to breathe without his permission. Losing your independence isn't worth the fame being with my father will bring you."

I feel my face burning. My breath catches in my throat. "How do you know?" I ask, but why do I even care how, when "why" should be the important question? Why does he intrude on my privacy?

"I keep a close eye on my children, and there are only a very few things I don't know about them, Lindsay. I wish you had been aware of it sooner. Your secret rendezvous with Ace is a breach of contract, but I will let it slip this time. Everyone is entitled to a mistake once, but I won't forgive the second time." He twists his arm to check his watch and then glances back at me. "I'm counting on you for next weekend. Keep your calendar empty. You're accompanying me as my date."

"I'm truly sorry, Michael, but for reasons I can't explain you, I can't attend the event next weekend. Please, understand that and don't insist."

He laughs, pushing back his chair, tossing his body against it. "Lindsay, my little, fake girlfriend. I think the time has come for you to start treating me as your boss and not some ordinary friend. I'm paying you two millions dollars. If I say, "you'll come to hell with me in two hours," I expect nothing but, "Yes, sir," as a response from you."

"With all due respect, that's a pretty high expectation. I have a life. I have obligations outside of my job."

"Well, you should have thought about your other commitments before taking up my offer. Now it's too late to use them as an excuse. You're coming with me. End of the discussion."

"Michael..." I start but he raises his hand to cut me off.

"You're not only expected to show up but also

fully assume your duties as my girlfriend."

"My duties as your girlfriend? What does that even mean?"

"Everything you imagine a man and woman in love would do in public to show their love, including but not limited to kissing and touching each other."

Ewww. My stomach twists at the thought of kissing him. "What? No way. I never agreed to that. In fact, I didn't even accept to be your pretend girlfriend. I only agreed to go out on dates with you. Nothing more. You'll never find such a term on the contract I signed."

"My dear, Lindsay. When will you finally grasp that the contract is a worthless piece of paper, and I do whatever I want with you regardless of what is written, or what's not on the contract."

I jump to my feet with anger and agitation. "Who do you think you are? You can't talk to me like that. I'm not your slave. If you think so little of the contract, it certainly doesn't carry any more importance for me, either. I'll pay back the money I received from you to the last cent and return the car. I'll send my resignation letter as soon as I'm out of your office," I yell before spinning on my heels and heading for the door.

My move will most likely damage Taylor's professional relationship with Michael, and I have no doubt Michael will try to hurt her company's reputation, but it's better that she's freed from another villain. She has a safety net of more than a hundred-million dollars that she inherited from her deceased first husband. It's not like she'll ever end up on the streets.

Just when I touch the doorknob, Michael says, "not so fast, young lady. I'm not done talking yet. You can leave only when I say you're dismissed, and I haven't yet said so."

"There's nothing else to talk about, Michael. I never felt comfortable getting into this agreement with you, and now I have enough confidence that it'd be best for us both if we call it off right now. Please, don't insist. You'll find a dozen willing girls more qualified to replace me for a tenth of the amount you paid me." I turn the doorknob and start to open it.

"Sit," he orders with a threatening tone, and I freeze on the spot. He stands, walks around his desk, and comes beside me to push the door closed. I notice a small device in his hand. It looks like a remote control. He points the device at a large TV attached to the wall and the images of Zane at my apartment fill the entire screen.

I watch myself in horror as I hand a glass of water to Zane. The next minutes are shocking enough to make me want to escape to the Brazilian jungles so I won't have to face anyone who might see me fucked by Zane over the arm of the couch. I look pathetic as I moan with Zane plunging into me.

I glance at Michael in disgust. My stomach revolts at the repulsive look on his face directed at me. Did he put cameras all around my apartment?

At one point, I'm recorded from front, at another Zane's back is seen. Which means there were two cameras, one close to the window in my living room, and the other on the other side of the room, both recording our fuck clearly and with no intrusion. Unless Michael is a detail freak and filled every corner of my apartment with dozens of cameras, it looks like the two cameras were set looking exactly at the arm of the couch. Not even the sitting part of couch itself. Then, I remember the suspicious way Zane asked me for water as soon as he'd entered my home. He might have set the cameras at that moment, when I was in the kitchen. That's why the recording starts with me handing him the water and not before.

And the coconut oil incident? That explains everything. It wasn't Ace who planned to use it to get to his brother. It was Zane, deliberately making himself go through an allergy attack so he can come over to my apartment, place video cameras, and fuck me while the cameras record every second of our depraved act. He wouldn't be able to do it at PE. Ace wouldn't allow him to protect my privacy. What a perfect set-up, now that I'm thinking about it. And, I let that happen. I allowed Zane to complete his plan without suspecting anything about his unusual arousal after having seen his tongue and half of his face swollen with an allergic reaction. Where was my mind? Who else goes from coming so close to death to having sex in a matter of an hour? Not someone with good intentions.

All the speeches Zane gave to warn me about Michael, and it turns out he was in it with him. Plotting ways to trap me into doing whatever Michael wants me to.

"Everyone has a weakness," Michael says over my moans coming from the TV. "And you delivered yours to me right away on the first day of our meeting. You, yourself, told me you can't go without men, and I just found a way to use that important piece of information to get what I want. Now, if you don't want to follow my orders, I'll make sure everyone in the world sees this. Not just that, the contract you signed with me will be leaked on the Internet before you can leave my office. Everyone will know what kind of a whore you are. Your life will be ruined, so will be your sister's."

"You promised me you wouldn't harm the project you have with Taylor's company."

"I don't need to do anything in particular for that. I'll just cancel the project, sit back, and watch how the word about their unprofessionalism spreads. It won't take more than a couple of months until she signs for bankruptcy. She'll lose everything she has. I just happened to learn that she donated her entire inheritance to charity half a year ago. I bet you'll agree with me about the stupidity of her move, considering the harsh unpredictability of the business environment. She won't have a back-up plan. She won't even be able to get a business loan. She'll be ruined for good."

Taylor gave away her millions? She hasn't told me anything about it, but it sounds like her.

Michael can't be lying about something I can find out easily with a phone call.

Oh, my goodness. The construction project Michael assigned to them was much bigger than Taylor's company had in the past. If Michael decides to pursue his threat, the cancellation of the contract in the middle of the project has the power to destroy everything she's worked for until now.

And, I'm pulling her down with me. Her company won't just have a bad reputation because of a canceled project, but also because of her whore of a sister, whose sex video will be all over the internet. She and her husband are both in the business together. They won't weep just for the death of their dead daughter, they'll break down entirely with the loss of their livelihood, too. What the hell have I done? I couldn't have dragged Taylor into more desperation even if I tried.

"Why? What do you want from me?" I ask, tears stinging my eyes. "I don't own any money besides what I received from you. I don't have access to highly confidential government data. I can't give you anything that you don't already have. What is it that you're ready to destroy me for?" I should have asked him these questions before signing the contract. Who else gives almost two million dollars to someone without an ulterior motive? But, what can it be that he wants from me?

He moves toward me, lifts his hand, and caresses my cheek. "Soon, my dear. You'll find it out very soon. But for now, I expect you to be at your best behavior for the next weekend, and you'll do everything to please my guests."

I work hard to swallow my disgust and not to yank his hand away. I'm ruined. I'm fucked, and nothing or no one can save me from the shit I pushed myself into. I played with the fire, enjoying its hotness, its bright colors, without caring about its dangers. I brought this upon me; I'll have to end it myself, even if it means I'll let a line of disgusting strangers fuck me over and over. Even if it means I'll become Michael's puppet and do as he pleases with me for as long as he wants. I have no other choice.

He glares at me, perhaps angry at my unresponsiveness. "I don't have the entire day. Give me your answer now. Julie is waiting for my word to upload the video and the contract on the internet. If you say no, your video will go online at this very second."

"Okay. I'll do whatever you want as long as

you don't hurt me or my sister."

"Deal."

"One more thing. You'll fucking stay clear of my children, including Ace. Your privileges at Pleasure Extraordinaire have just ended. If I find out that you're anywhere around that building except for when I order it, I'll consider it a reason to end our deal."

I won't see Ace anymore? I won't get to kiss him again, wrap my arms around his comforting body? Pain slashes through my body at the thought of the lonely days ahead of me without Ace soothing my pain, giving me courage to move on, and look ahead despite Michael. Worse than the thought of having the world witness how Zane fucked me. I close my eyes, willing my tears to not leave my eyes, and simply nod my acceptance.

"Now you're dismissed."

I turn toward the door, dragging my heavy body as I open it and walk through it, cursing the first day I entered through this very doorway. How foolish and naïve I was for believing in the idea of having my life changed with a seemingly profitable contract. Tears rolls down my cheeks freely as I rush through Julie's office. Just when I reach the exit door, I see her smirking at me with contempt. She must have seen my video and be thinking what a slut I am. Everyone else will have the same opinion of me if Michael puts the video and the contract online.

I'm trapped, living the end of my life as I know it. I'll have to pray that it won't get any worse than this, but something inside me is telling me this is just the beginning.

THE END

ABOUT THE AUTHOR

Liv Bennett lives in California with her scientist husband, toddler daughter, and two loud budgies. Reading and writing erotic romance are her favorite forms of relaxation, in addition to long walks and yoga. She's a social drinker of coffee but a serious tea addict.

Sign up to get alerts about her upcoming releases

eepurl.com/F_nqD
www.facebook.com/LivBennettAuthor
slivbennett@gmail.com

***

Other books by Liv Bennett

An Illicit Pursuit (PURSUIT #1)

The Pursuit of Passion (PURSUIT #2)

An Everlasting Pursuit (PURSUIT #3)

Pleasure Extraordinaire #1 (PURSUIT #4)

Pleasure Extraordinaire #2 (PURSUIT #4)

Pleasure Extraordinaire #3 (PURSUIT #4)

56870815R00145

Made in the USA
Columbia, SC
02 May 2019